Shadow of a Star

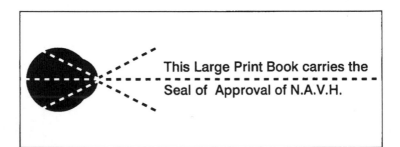

This Large Print Book carries the
Seal of Approval of N.A.V.H.

Shadow

of a

STAR

ELMER KELTON

G.K. Hall & Co. • Thorndike, Maine

Published in 2000 by arrangement with Sobel Weber Associates, Inc.

G.K. Hall Large Print Western Series.

The text of this Large Print edition is unabridged.
Other aspects of the book may vary from the original edition.

Set in 16 pt. Plantin.

Printed in the United States on permanent paper.

Library of Congress Cataloging-in-Publication Data

Kelton, Elmer.
    Shadow of a star / Elmer Kelton.
       p.   cm.
    ISBN 0-7838-8946-1 (lg. print : hc : alk. paper)
    1. Large type books.   I. Title.
  PS3561.E3975 S47   2000
   813´.54—dc21   99-086902

Shadow of a Star

Chapter One

They had shaken the last sign of pursuit two days ago. Now they had to stop riding, for Curly Jack was dying on their hands.

They eased him to the warm ground beneath the thin shade of a mesquite. Because the sun still came through, Dencil Fox unsaddled Curly Jack's horse and draped the wet saddle blanket across the branches to deepen the shade. Dencil poured water from a canteen into a handkerchief and gently touched it to Jack's fevered face.

"You just need to rest a spell, pardner," he said. "You'll be all right directly."

But he knew he was lying. There was the smell of gangrene about Curly Jack — the smell of death.

He wondered how Jack had managed to stay in the saddle as long as he had. It wasn't such a bad wound, they had thought. A bullet high in the shoulder, nothing fatal. But they hadn't dared hunt for a doctor. And the posse hadn't given them much chance to probe for the bullet the first couple of days. When at last they'd had time for Dencil to try, he hadn't been able to extract the slug. If anything, his efforts had made things worse.

Jack weakly motioned toward the canteen, and Dencil touched it to his lips, lifting Jack's head.

The other three men stood around uncomfortably, a deep weariness in their eyes, the droop of their shoulders. They were dusty and bearded. The oldest two were silent, but the youngest began to complain.

"We could have left him off someplace the first day. They'd have found him and took care of him."

Dencil Fox frowned quickly at his younger brother, then looked back at Curly Jack. "They'd have taken care of him, all right. Jack had rather go this way than at the end of a rope.

"If he was goin' to die anyhow, at least we wouldn't have been saddled down with him."

Sharply Dencil said, "Shut up, Buster!" He knew Curly Jack could still hear all that was said.

Buster kept talking. "If he'd shot that bank teller, he wouldn't have caught a slug himself."

Dencil said, "We didn't go in there to kill anybody."

"You *didn't* kill anybody. And you didn't get any money, either."

"We didn't figure on that gutty teller. And we never did know where he got that gun so fast."

Buster Fox said bitterly, "Leavin' me outside to hold the horses . . . If I'd been in there, things would've been a right smart different."

"That's why we left you outside."

"Well, you won't leave me outside next time!"

Curly Jack died without ever speaking a word.

Because there was no shovel, they had to carry him to an arroyo, roll him in his saddle blanket, and cave a steep bank in on top of him. This way, at least, no one was likely to find him for a while. Later, if a rise came down the arroyo and washed the body out into the open, the four riders would be so far gone that the discovery would not put them in danger.

Dencil Fox stood with hat in hand, gravely looking down on the pile of fresh-caved earth at the bottom of the arroyo.

"Mighty poor way to leave you, Jack." His voice was sorrowful. "No marker, no preacher to read over you."

Buster spoke dryly, "Jack wasn't exactly the church-goin' kind."

Dencil said, "He was a good man, and don't you forget it."

"Too bad he wasn't a good shot."

They rode on then, leading Jack's horse for an extra, putting miles between them and the place where the fifth outlaw had died.

In time Dencil Fox said, "We got to find us a good spot to lay over. These horses will die under us if we don't rest them a few days."

A tall rider named Hackberry said, "We crossed the railroad tracks late yesterday. I figure we're about halfway between Grafton and Swallowfork. There's a big draw runs through a ways this side of Swallowfork. With the wet spring they had here, there ought to be good grass in it, and plenty of water. We could camp there as long as we wanted. Ain't anybody apt to see us except maybe a stray cowpuncher or two."

Dencil said, "You don't reckon they've heard about that bank job?"

"That was a long ways off. Last time I was in Swallowfork, it didn't have no telegraph or nothin'. Who'd be lookin' for us down here?"

"Nobody, I reckon. And I could sure use me a good rest."

The younger Fox pushed his horse up close to Hackberry's. "What kind of a town is this Swallowfork? Chance a man could find himself a little entertainment?"

Hackberry said, "The kind you're lookin' for?" He shook his head. "Last time I was there it was just a dull lookin' little cowtown. You could get yourself somethin' to drink and maybe a quiet game of cards, low limit. Nothin' fancy. And no wheeligo girls."

Buster was plainly disappointed. "Ain't that a shame!" Then, his face brightened again. "I wonder if they got a bank . . ."

A loud clatter was going on at the shack's old cast-iron cookstove.

"If you don't quit polishin' that tin star and go chop some firewood, there won't be any breakfast!"

Sitting on the edge of his cot, Jim-Bob McClain turned about with a youthfully sheepish grin and waved a hand at the young man who had spoken. "Hold your horses, Dan.

10

I'll get to it directly." He pinned the deputy badge on his left shirt pocket, catching the Bull Durham sack with the pin the first time he tried. He reached down and pulled on his long-eared, high-heeled boots. He already had his hat on. It was the first thing he looked for when he got up of a morning: an old cowboy habit he had developed sleeping on the ground in wintertime, dressing from the head downward as he worked up out of the warm blankets.

Dan Singleton stood at the black stove, poking remnant woodchips in on top of the reluctant flame he coaxed out of dry kindling. Ashes filtered out around the sprung door and fell at his feet. "Thought this was your week to chop the wood," Dan prodded Jim-Bob good-naturedly. "Or do I have to call out the law?"

"I meant to do it last night, but with the dance down at Sothern's barn and all, I flat forgot."

"Then you better get at it, or it's goin' to be a long, hungry day."

Jim-Bob walked out of the little frame shack and paused to enjoy the clean freshness of the early morning. This was the summertime's best hour in the West Texas range country, just at sunup. The cool air of a brand new day braced a man and gave him vigor, made him imagine he could ride horseback a hundred miles without his shoulders ever sagging. It gave him all manner of grand ambition, notions the noonday heat would later bake out of him.

Along the wagon road just hollering distance

away lay the beginnings of the town of Swallowfork. A scattering of frame and adobe houses first, thickening up and bunching closer together the nearer they lay to the rock court-house and jail and the dozen or so business buildings that made up the core, it sprawled out haphazardly like a big *remuda* of horses loose-herded across half of a valley.

Jim-Bob listened. About all he could hear was a couple of roosters crowing the sun up, and a shut-in milkpen calf bawling for its mammy.

Quiet town, most of the time. Sleepy livestock town, drawing its livelihood from the good rolling rangeland that lay about it; from the tall bunch grasses that made the hillsides wave green in the gentle south breeze; from the valley's short, tough curly-mesquite buffalo grass; from the leggy, longhorned cattle that roamed and grazed there; and from the scattering bands of free-ranging sheep that were edging in on the cowman's domain, winning him over by pressure of economics if not from liking for the animal.

Quiet town it was, but one with ambitions, and one with a future. Jim-Bob's town. Like the town, he had ambitions. He could only hope *he* had a future, too.

He stood with hands shoved deep in his pockets, jingling the coins he carried there. Pay from his first month as a deputy sheriff of Cold-ridge County. He had hoped and worked and planned for a long time to pin that badge on his shirt. Now he had it.

"Jim-Bob," Dan Singleton's impatient voice insisted through the open door, "how about that wood?"

"Comin'."

A big red dog, ugly as a mud fence, sidled around the shack and came up wagging his tail. "Mornin', Ranger," Jim-Bob greeted him, patting his broad head. "Where'd you spend the night? Liable to be a scandal around here if you don't take to stayin' home."

Jim-Bob unwedged the ax from the big mesquite limb that served as a chopping block and pulled a smaller limb down from the woodpile. He and Dan Singleton had taken a couple of Sunday afternoons and a borrowed wagon to haul in this supply of dry wood from a brushy draw a ways out of town. His strong back and hard-muscled arms made short work of the wood. In a few minutes he walked into the shack with a good armload.

"Hope you didn't cut it too long this time," Dan said. He had once accused Jim-Bob of trying to do such a poor job of it that Dan would take over in disgust. He wasn't far wrong. Jim-Bob never did go much for wood-chopping and the like. He preferred something he could do a-horseback. But a man who made up his mind to live in town and be a deputy sheriff also had to make up his mind to do some menial chores he didn't care for.

Outside for another armload of wood, Jim-

Bob paused to squint down the south wagon road that led in from Dry Creek and from ranches like the C Bar. There, in the reddish glow of the sun just up, he saw two riders trotting their horses purposefully toward town. Recognizing them, he waved.

"You-all come on over and have breakfast with us," he called.

They only acknowledged his offer with a quick wave of their hands and rode on. By the rigid way they sat their saddles, Jim-Bob could tell they meant business. He frowned and looked down at rusty-hided old Ranger, who had moved out a little way to size up the pair. "Somethin' the matter, Ranger. They've had to ride half the night to get in from the C Bar. And they're both packin' guns."

The way the country had settled up and closed in, folks weren't wearing their guns much anymore. When they did, it was usually because they felt a genuine need for them.

"Now what would Walter Chapman and Tom Singleton be needin' with guns?" he mused.

Walter Chapman owned the C Bar. Tom Singleton was his foreman and Dan Singleton's older brother.

Jim-Bob had worked on Chapman's ranch for several years after his father had died and left the growing boy to shift for himself. Excepting maybe Sheriff Mont Naylor, there wasn't a better man to work for, anywhere, than Walter Chapman. He was a solid old ranchman of the

14

longhorn school. When he said work, now, he meant *work,* but he'd be right there beside you, or maybe out in front of you. He paid well and never abused man or horse. Always an easy mark for a hard-luck story, he was forever picking up dogies like the orphaned Singleton boys or Jim-Bob McClain, giving them a chance to work out their own way. But if he ever caught you lying to him or cheating him, there would be hell among the yearlings.

Dan Singleton stood in the door, watching the riders move on toward town. "That looked like Tom," he said, puzzled.

Jim-Bob went on picking up wood. "It was him. Never even stopped to say howdy."

"Awfully early for him to be in town. Must be something wrong out there."

"I reckon we'll hear about it soon enough." Heavily loaded, Jim-Bob strained to pick up the one remaining piece of wood and spilled half of his armload. He muttered something under his breath and made two trips of it.

He had the woodbox half full by the time Dan called him. He brushed the dust and chips away from his clothes and poured fresh water into a basin on the soap-slick washstand. Lathering his hands as best he could in the strong soap, he took a long whiff of the bacon-and-black coffee smell. Dan was a heap sight better cook than Jim-Bob ever even wanted to be.

Jim-Bob liked Dan, and he liked this place they shared here on the edge of town: an ancient

15

shack, a small barn, a couple of corrals and a creaky windmill that needed new leathers and a greasing. The shack wasn't much, as houses go. They had painted it inside and out, but the job had been done several years too late to keep the place from weathering beyond redemption. One corner sagged gently where the cedar-post foundation had sunk. The windows didn't fit well anymore, and the west wind whistled in around them. The roof leaked in a couple of places, but this was a dry country where a leaky roof was only an occasional inconvenience. For two happy young bachelors in the springtime of life and the first glow of real independence, the place was more than adequate.

Dan Singleton was getting a good start as a teller in the bank. He'd always been a good-enough kid cowboy, but it had been easy to tell that he held promise of better things. He liked to read, and he had an unusual aptitude with figures. There wasn't an old-time cowman around who could do a better job of tallying cattle. Dan never dropped a count. Walter Chapman had finally fired him off the C Bar for his own good, forcing him to accept the job which old man True Farrell had been offering him at the bank. Dan Singleton was going to amount to something someday, people said. And everybody knew that one of the things West Texas needed most was more bankers who knew something about the cow business.

They weren't all sure about Jim-Bob McClain.

He was a pretty fair cowboy, a little on the wild side. He would ride any horse they led out to him, or at least would try to. He would rope anything that would run from him, and he would stand tied to it. But he would never make a banker, or a storekeeper. Most people figured he would just end up another stove-up cowpuncher.

But old John McClain before him had been sheriff of Coldridge County for many years, and a good one. Sheriff Mont Naylor had the idea that young Jim-Bob McClain might have the makings in him, too, if he had a little of the rashness stomped out of him. Jim-Bob had pestered him long enough about it, anyway.

Jim-Bob's chance came when Mont had to fire Chum Lawton for pistol-whipping a harmless old Mexican sheepherder whose only crime had been taking on a little too much tequila. Mont rode out to the C Bar and swore Jim-Bob in.

If he lived a hundred years, Jim-Bob would never again know the great swell of pride that came when Mont pinned the deputy's badge on him.

Yesterday was a month he'd worn that badge. "Here's for your first month," Mont had spoken simply as he paid him. And that was all he had said. Not a thank you or a howdydo, just that and nothing more. The young deputy had tried to see something more in the sheriff's eyes, for nothing in the world mattered like pleasing Mont Naylor. He listened to those five words a hundred times in his mind, and still he didn't know. He had done his best. Maybe that hadn't been enough.

Good thing about living close to town this way, they could always buy fresh food like vegetables and eggs, something they had often missed on the ranch. Jim-Bob liked his eggs. He was so busy eating that he didn't pay much attention to Dan Singleton. He finally noticed Dan watching him with humor in his eyes.

"You were sure havin' a good time at the dance," Dan said.

"Had to stay around and be sure things stayed peaceful. It's what I'm hired for."

"I think you were goin' far beyond the call of duty. I noticed you takin' mighty good care of Tina Kendrick. You never gave anybody else much chance to dance with her."

Jim-Bob felt his face coloring. It had never occurred to him that anybody would notice. Looking away from Dan, he dropped a strip of bacon into Ranger's eager jaws.

Dan said, "Chum Lawton was plenty burned up. After all, he brought her, and you danced with her all night."

His dancing with Tina Kendrick wasn't all that had Chum Lawton riled, Jim-Bob thought. There never had been much love lost between them, and especially not since Jim-Bob got Chum's old job. Chum was out breaking tough broncs for a living now. It wasn't something a man enjoyed after soft living around town.

18

Dan commented, "That little girl, Sue-Ellen Thorn, from up the creek, had her eyes on you a lot. You could have her, I think, if you wanted her."

Jim-Bob grunted. "I was scared to death she was goin' to come right out and ask me to dance. You know, they tell me there's girls that will do things like that."

Dan shook his head, smiling. "Must be awful tough to have so many girls on the string."

Sheriff Mont Naylor rode up as Jim-Bob carried his dirty dishes to the washpan on the kitchen cabinet. Walter Chapman and Tom Singleton sat beside him on their horses, their faces grim.

The sheriff said, "If you've finished breakfast, Jim-Bob, you better go saddle your horse. We got a job to do."

Jim-Bob didn't like the undertone of worry in the sheriff's voice. He looked at Walter and Tom, expecting one of them to offer an explanation. They didn't. Well, they would tell him in their own due time, he figured.

"You fellers get down and come on in," he said. "There's still coffee on the stove."

Dan Singleton stepped to the door, his face brightening as he looked out at his older brother. They quietly shook hands. No words passed between them, for sometimes brothers know little to say to each other. Just being together was enough.

Tom Singleton was tall and stiff-backed, a

severe man who looked older than his thirty years. He wore a black vest and a black moustache and a solemn mien that he never relaxed. He wasn't an easy man to get to know, but there was this about him: he was honest and worked hard, and he had little patience with anyone who did not. To him, black was black and white was white. People knew that, and they respected him for it whether they agreed with him or not.

Only one thing ever softened Tom Singleton's eyes. Talk about his younger brother Dan and you could see a glow of pride start there. Tom Singleton had been in his teens when the responsibility for Dan had been thrust upon him. Tom had worked harder than two men, had missed the happy, youthful years to which he himself was entitled. But Dan had borne out all his hope, had justified all his sacrifice. Tom might never speak of his pride, but it showed in his dark eyes.

Jim-Bob walked to the little barn out back, Ranger following along with his stumpy tail twitching. Most of the time they let the horses run free on the town-section grass when they weren't using them. Everybody did. They made it a point to feed a little grain first thing after breakfast every morning, rain or shine. That guaranteed that the mounts would always be up in case they needed them.

The sheriff and Walter Chapman came around in a minute. Looping his bridle reins over a post, the sheriff felt of the rough bark on a big mesquite tree to be sure there wasn't any sticky sap on it. Then he squatted stiffly and leaned his back against it, grunting with the effort. At his age, and with his growing weight, his knees popped when he bent very far.

People in Coldridge County always said they'd been blessed with good sheriffs. John McClain had set a strong pattern. He had usually found a peaceful way to handle the problems that came up. But when something demanded rough treatment, McClain had been able to administer it.

Mont Naylor was an old-time cowman, like John McClain before him. He had brought his own herd up with him from the brush of southern Texas in the early days and had settled in the upper end of the county. Eventually, drought and low prices got a stranglehold on him and left him flat broke. But people didn't want to see him go. Because Mont Naylor had always been a good horse trader, banker True Farrell lent him money to buy out the Swallowfork livery barn and wagonyard. Later, when John McClain died, folks prevailed on Mont to take over as sheriff on a temporary basis. It was the longest temporary job he'd ever had.

Mont was a broad-shouldered, deep-chested man with a square face hard-bitten by a lifetime in the hot, dry wind and the sullen punishment of the Texas sun. The creases in his face, always deep enough, bit even deeper this morning as he frowned over the trouble that had brought him here.

Jim-Bob itched to ask what they were going to do, but he had learned better years ago as a kid around a cow camp. The button who asked a lot of fool questions would find himself jingling horses, holding the cut or trotting the mountain oysters back to camp for the wagon cook.

Jim-Bob noted that the sheriff had his saddlegun along. It was the first time he had carried it since Jim-Bob had been working for him. Mont sat with his back to the mesquite, his lips puffed out while he worried. He absently sketched cattle brands in the sand and then changed them over the way a rustler would. Mont had seen it all done in his time.

Presently Mont said, "We're goin' out to Jace Dunnigan's. We all know he's been butcherin' C bar beef. This time Walter and Tom think they can prove it on him."

That was no great surprise to Jim-Bob. Jace Dunnigan had a ratty little place some distance from town. He kept a few cattle, bought a few occasionally, and — it was generally believed — stole a lot more than he bought. Jace supplied beef to a good many townspeople. Though it was basic knowledge that there were but four quarters to a beef, it was a common joke around Swallowfork that Dunnigan cattle grew seven or eight apiece.

Mont said, "Tom Singleton spotted him yesterday out on the C Bars, nosin' around just a little before dark. He followed him and saw him pick up a fat heifer yearlin'. He trailed Jace right

22

on to his place. Jace killed the heifer, skinned it and buried the hide a little ways from the house. Tom says he's sure he can find that hide this mornin'."

Jim-Bob pointed his chin at the sheriff's saddlegun. "You don't think you'll need that thing with a man like Jace . . ."

"You never can tell."

Jim-Bob walked back into the shack and strapped on his gun. It was a single-action Colt Frontier .44 with black rubber grips. John McClain had left his son little but a gold pocket-watch, a fond memory, and this heavy old six-shooter.

Nobody did much talking as they rode out. To Jim-Bob it was as if they were going to a funeral. He tried to make conversation, but he soon realized he was the only one doing any talking. As the youngest, he knew it behooved him to shut up, and he did.

They rode back south down the wagon trail, toward the C Bar. Jim-Bob watched Tom Singleton as they rode. It struck him that Tom would always be the standout in whatever crowd he might ride, his back so rigid that it made anyone else look slovenly beside him. He was a handsome man, even in his severity, with steady brown eyes almost black, a straight nose, and that strong black moustache. He wore a flat-brimmed gray hat, its tall crown barely pinched toward the top. Even in dusty ranch clothes he always seemed better dressed than the

23

others around him.

Tom Singleton had been known to go for days without saying anything other than the bare necessities for getting the work done. On roundup, he usually took the lead and rode a length or two ahead of the other men as he led them around the outer part of the circle to drop them off for the drive. Even now, he rode a little ahead of Mont Naylor and Walter Chapman.

The men's silence was not broken until they happened across a calf that showed a wound infested by screwworms. The calf carried someone else's brand, but it was unthinkable that it should be left to die untreated simply because it belonged to another man.

Tom Singleton shook down his rope, built a small loop and gently edged toward the calf. He took it slow and easy, easing the calf a little way from its mother. At the crucial moment when the calf suddenly turned to bolt, Tom touched rowels to the horse. The loop swung around his head only once, then dropped like a rock and fitted perfectly over the calf's neck. No sweat, no strain, the way Tom Singleton did things. Jim-Bob watched with admiration. Dan Singleton had always been his pal, but Tom had been his ideal. Tom was a cowboy for you, now. Anything he set out to do, he would do it better than anyone else.

The calf's mammy was bawling and working around with her head low, trying to get up the courage to charge in. Jim-Bob moved to keep her away while Tom was down pouring chloroform into the wound. Freed at last, the calf ran to her. With all the concern a mother can show, the cow sniffed around on it to be sure it was all right. Then she shook her head threateningly at the riders, turned and trotted away with the calf.

Somehow the incident loosened up Tom Singleton a little. He said nothing, but he winked at Jim-Bob as he swung back onto his horse. It loosened Walter Chapman a little, too. He seemed to feel a need to explain the reason for this ride out to Dunnigan's. "It's not as if he was some hungry nester, Mont, butcherin' a beef once in a while for his young'uns. They've done it many a time, and I've never said a word. But Jace Dunnigan's been killin' our cattle for sale, stickin' the money in his pocket and gettin' drunk on it. He could find him an honest job if he was a mind to. He's just too sorry to do anything but drink and steal."

The sheriff nodded. "The state'll find him a nice permanent job over at Huntsville, I expect. There he'll sweat or go hungry."

There wasn't an adobe hovel in the west end of town that looked half as bad as Jace Dunnigan's place. He lived like a boar hog in a swaying frame shack that had cardboard in place of half the glass windows. A scattering of tin cans and old bottles made a horseshoe-shaped pile out behind the house. The rustiest ones lay the farthest away, indicating that the junkpile was edging closer to the house as the man got lazier.

Tom Singleton reined up. He hadn't spoken since they had left town. Now he said, "Right there, I think it was, Mont. See the dried mud on some of those cans? He buried the hide under there and kicked the cans over to hide the fresh dirt."

Jim-Bob caught a movement at one of the dirty windows. "Somebody in the shack," he said. The head bobbed and was gone. "Looked like a woman."

"Mrs. Dunnigan," Mont replied.

Walter Chapman nodded. "I saw her. Always puzzled me, why a woman would live like this, in the midst of all the filth, with the likes of Jace Dunnigan."

Jim-Bob shook his head. "No woman could love a man like that."

Mont glanced his way. "You're too young to know much about women, son." He paused, then added, "I wonder if any man ever gets old enough."

"Do you really think a woman could love a man who makes her live like this?"

Mont shrugged. "I've seen fine women fall in love with men that weren't fit to breathe the same air. I've seen good men go plumb out of their heads and fall into the mud over some common dancehall floozy. You just take a good look, Jim-Bob, and let it be a lesson to you."

A brown mongrel dog crept out from under the shack and set up a racket. His ribs showed like bed slats through his coarse hide. Sheriff Mont Naylor stepped down out of the saddle, careful to keep his horse between himself and the house as he did so.

"Jace," he called. "Jace Dunnigan."

Jim-Bob stayed in the saddle, hand close to the old gun on his hip. Excitement kindled in him. This was the first time in his month as a deputy that he faced even the remote possibility of using a gun. He watched the front door. Jace Dunnigan might be inside, or he might not. But Mrs. Dunnigan was there. He wondered why she didn't answer.

The dog kept on barking. Presently Jace Dunnigan walked around the corner of the house. He reached down and picked up a rock. "Gil!" be shouted at the mongrel. He hurled the stone, striking the dog so hard that Jim-Bob flinched at the flat *whu-u-mp* of the rock against bare ribs. Yelping, the dog tucked its tail between its legs and slunk back under the house.

Jace Dunnigan turned then to his visitors. His yellowed teeth — what there were left of them — protruded a little. His lips were perpetually pulled back, his mouth open. He stood slackly, lank shoulders drooping. His clothes were filthy with grease and dried animal blood. Jim-Bob could smell him from six feet away.

Jim-Bob wondered suddenly how many times he had eaten beef butchered by this dirty man. The thought made him a little sick.

"Howdy, Mont," Jace said lazily. His red-veined eyes flicked to the other three men without any particular friendliness, for he knew full well what Walter Chapman and Tom Singleton thought of him, and Jim-Bob was just a big kid who didn't matter. Puzzlement came into Jace's eyes, and a trace of worry. But he tried to cover it up.

"I got a little shot of whisky out at the barn," he said by way of invitation.

Mont replied evenly, "I don't think I'd care for any right now. But I *would* like to take a look around that barn. I reckon you got some beef hangin' up?"

Suspicion narrowed Jace's eyes. "Matter of fact, I butchered one of my calves last night. Got the beef in the barn, coolin' out. Figured I'd haul it into town this evenin' when the heat of the day was past."

"Mind if we look at it?"

Dunnigan hesitated. Then, voice lower, he said, "I don't see as it would hurt nothin'." He looked uneasily at Walter Chapman. His glance barely touched Tom Singleton, then flicked away. Tom's dark eyes were boring a hole through him, loathing him for the sneak thief that he was.

Dunnigan led the way out to the barn. A couple of thin calves stood waiting pathetically beside an empty feed trough. It would be a long time before these were ever fat enough to butcher.

The beef, sawed down the spine, hung in two

halves on rope suspended from a sagging rafter. There was no tarp cover. Flies buzzed around.

Jim-Bob felt his stomach turn over.

Mont Naylor nodded in satisfaction. This carcass was a lot fatter than any cattle Jim-Bob had ever seen wearing Jace's brand. Mont said, "Where's the hide off of this animal, Jace?"

A tremor was beginning in Jace's voice. "Why, I hung it out over a corral fence." He showed them a hide, laid flesh side up. Dry and stiff as a board, it hadn't come from any fresh-killed animal. Jace said, "The brand's right there if you want to turn the hide over and read it. My brand, Mont, you can see for yourself."

Mont paid little attention to him. He poked around a little and found a shovel. He held it out to Tom Singleton. "Go see if you can find that hide you were talkin' about."

Jace Dunnigan seemed to wilt as he watched Tom Siingleton walk toward the pile of rusty cans, the shovel in his hand. Sweat popped out on his forehead. His tongue worked constantly back and forth over his lips. His hands shook as he took a tooth-marked cut of plug tobacco out of his pocket and tried to chew it. He spat it out in a moment, still as dry as when he had stuck it in his mouth.

His wife moved out onto the back step of the house, watching. She was a thin, pale woman with hair almost completely gray. Yet she couldn't have been forty years old, Jim-Bob reasoned. He thought he could see a dark bruise marring her face. Life with Jace Dunnigan was far from easy.

Tom Singleton dropped to one knee and began to scoop out dirt with one of the rusty cans. He stood up again and came back, dragging a dirty hide by the tail. It was still soft and pliable.

"Looks fresh, Jace," Mont commented quietly. "Last night fresh."

Glaring at Dunnigan, Tom dropped the tail and toed the bloody hide over, revealing the brand. "There you are, Mont. C Bar."

Jace Dunnigan trembled. He cleared his throat. "Now looky here, Mont, maybe I made a little mistake."

"I reckon you did."

"It was gettin' dark," Dunnigan argued desperately. "I thought it was mine till I had it shot. It was too late then, and you wouldn't want me to let that meat go to spoil. It's the first time it ever happened."

Seeing Mont didn't accept that, Dunnigan turned to Walter Chapman. "Look, Mr. Chapman, tell you what I'll do. I'll give you one of them calves yonder for it. Fair swap, even up. What you say?"

"I say you're a dirty liar. I say you've killed more C Bar cattle than my whole crew could brand in a day. And now you're fixin' to pay for every one of them."

Sick fear was in Jace Dunnigan's red eyes. Not many years ago, he would probably have been hauled out to the nearest tree, had a rope put around his neck, and a wagon rolled out from under him.

Jim-Bob figured that thought was running through Dunnigan's mind.

Jace's voice quavered. "Mont, what you goin' to do?"

"Goin' to take you in, Jace. Try you, ship you off to Huntsville penitentiary for six or eight years."

"Penitentiary." The word came off Dunnigan's lips in a dreading whisper. "Ohmigod, Mont, no." He was shaking like a thin dog in a cold rain.

Mont Naylor looked levelly at him. "I wish I could say I'm sorry, Jace, but I can't. Fact of the matter, I don't know as I ever enjoyed an arrest more. Jim-Bob, come over here and put your handcuffs on him."

Jim-Bob moved up with the cuffs. He had never seen a man in a spot like this before. For a moment he felt a tug of sympathy, looking into the hopeless eyes of this miserable thief. "Let's see the hands, Jace."

Dunnigan lifted his shaking hands. Jim-Bob got one cuff on him, but he found he was almost as nervous as Dunnigan. He had accidentally locked the other cuff. He looked around, fishing in his pocket for the key. The instant he felt the gun jerked from his holster, he knew he had made a mistake.

Dunnigan pushed him hard. Caught off balance, Jim-Bob landed on his hands and knees and rolled in the dirt.

Dunnigan stepped back, the .44 gripped tightly in both hands, the one loose cuff dangling. "Just you hold still now, Mont," he said excitedly. His eyes were wild. "You ain't sendin' me off to no pen to rot. I never stole enough cattle to break anybody."

Mont Naylor was caught by surprise, but his voice was still even and strong with authority. "You're makin' it harder on yourself, Jace. Be sensible and put that gun down. You let it go off and it won't be just cow stealin' anymore. They'll hang you for murder."

Mont took a step forward. Jace steadied his hands, and for a second it looked as if he was going to fire. Jim-Bob lay frozen in fear for Mont.

Mont said, "I'm givin' you just one more chance, Jace. You can't get away, so don't hurt yourself any more than you already are. Drop the gun."

Dunnigan held it, retreating another step. Mont started to move forward, pressing him. Dunnigan's eyes widened in wild resolution, and his finger went tight on the trigger.

Mont threw himself to the ground, drawing his own gun as he fell. The .44 roared in Dunnigan's hands, but Mont already had dropped beneath the path of the bullet. Mont squeezed his trigger just once.

Dunnigan doubled over as if hit by a sledge.

He went to his knees, groaned once, then pitched forward in a loose heap.

Jim-Bob still lay where he had fallen. For a moment all the strength seemed to be drained out of him. He couldn't even get up. In that last instant of life, Jace Dunnigan had looked straight at Jim-Bob. Jim-Bob clenched his fists and squinched his own eyes shut as if the pain had been his. Never, as long as he lived, would he forget the mortal fear and agony he had seen in Jace Dunnigan. And it had been Jim-Bob's fault. Shame flooded him.

Deadly silence followed for a long moment that stretched like eternity. Then a woman's voice lifted in a wail. Mrs. Dunnigan came, screaming as she ran. She threw herself down across the slack body and squalled.

As a precaution, Tom Singleton leaned over and picked up Jim-Bob's gun that Dunnigan had dropped. Then he helped the young deputy to his feet, his dark eyes asking if Jim-Bob was all right. Jim-Bob only nodded. His throat was drawn up in such a tight knot that he couldn't speak. The men stood helplessly watching the woman. They looked at each other, and no man had any suggestion. Mont Naylor tried to put his hand comfortingly on her thin shoulder, but she jerked away from him, eyes ablaze in hatred.

"Murderers!" she screamed. "Murderers!"

Jim-Bob could tell now that he had been right about the bruises on her face. One eye was swollen half shut. How, he asked himself, could a woman carry on so about the death of a husband like that? The wonder was that she hadn't killed him herself.

To Tom Singleton he said tightly, "Looks to me like she's better off with him dead."

Tom told him what he knew he should have seen for himself. "She's simple, Jim-Bob. She's got the mind of a child. He could beat her and starve her, and still she stayed with him because she was afraid to be alone. Now she *is* alone."

Mont Naylor stood white-faced and shaken. Only then did Jim-Bob fully realize how this had affected him. Mont was the kind of man who would lose many a night's sleep, seeing Jace Dunnigan die again and again.

"I'm sorry, Mont," he said. "It was my fault you had to do it."

Mont looked through him as if he didn't see him. Then he said quietly, "There's a wagon out back of the barn. Go see if you can find his team and catch them up. We'll take him to town."

Chapter Two

Jace Dunnigan's funeral was an awful ordeal to Jim-Bob McClain. The one good thing about it, it didn't last very long. Almost no one was there. Just the widow, the minister, Mont Naylor, Jim-Bob and a couple of the elder town leaders who went only out of sympathy for the widow.

Walking back alone from the graveyard on the hill, Jim-Bob could feel people watching him. He thought he knew what was running through their minds. It wouldn't have happened if this wet-eared deputy hadn't been careless.

Some of the townsmen quietly made up a collection for Mrs. Dunnigan. Jim-Bob stood off at a distance, miserable, and watched her board the mail hack for Grafton. She wore a plain black dress that some thoughtful woman had given her, for she had owned nothing fit to travel in. At Grafton she would catch a train and return to her own people in East Texas.

Jim-Bob leaned against a porch post in front of the bank, savagely whittling down a piece of white pine with the sharp blade of his pocket-knife. Feeling a hand touch his shoulder, he looked around at Dan Singleton.

"Stop blamin' yourself, Jim-Bob. You didn't

sleep last night, and you haven't eaten. You know she's better off with him dead. Maybe he's better off too. He'd probably have died in that pen."

Jim-Bob nodded bleakly. "I reckon so. But still, he'd be alive now if I hadn't pulled that stupid stunt and let him get ahold of my gun. Mont Naylor wouldn't have him on his conscience, either."

"Has Mont said he blames you?"

Jim-Bob looked down. "He hasn't said anything at all. He doesn't have to."

Dan's voice was quiet but sincere. "I make a mistake at the bank once in a while, but True Farrell doesn't blame me for it. He says the best lessons you learn are through the mistakes you make. I don't ever make the same one twice. Neither will you."

"None of your mistakes ever cause a man to die."

"Mine's not that kind of a job. Yours is."

Jim-Bob sat down on the edge of the high porch and flipped the pine stick away. He absently thumbed the point of the knifeblade. "It may not be my job very long. Old man Trumpett and a couple of the merchants were in to see Mont this mornin'. I reckon they wanted me to hear every word they said. They told him I was too much of a kid for a job like this. Told him he ought to fire me and get somebody with enough experience to wear a badge right and proper. Maybe hire back Chum Lawton."

"What did Mont say?"

"I skipped out while Trumpett was still talkin'. But I expect they were right, and Mont knows it. He'll get around to tellin' me in his own good time."

Dan listened sympathetically. At length he said, "Maybe not, Jim-Bob. But if he does —" he hesitated a moment "— this isn't the only town in West Texas. We could go off, you and me, and we'd find something."

"Dan, you've got a fine job here."

Dan shrugged. "What're partners for? We've been partners a long time."

Jim-Bob swallowed. He remembered what his father had told him years ago about friends being worth more than any amount of money. He hadn't been able to figure that one then. But he could see it now. He shook his head. "You're not goin' to leave here, Dan. I'm not goin' to stand for that."

He walked on down to the jail and found Mont there. Only one prisoner had spent the night in the jail. He was a cowboy who had been breaking up furniture and bottles at a little adobe *cantina* on the west end last night, trying to pick a fight with the Mexicans. Jim-Bob had tried to stop him, but the cowboy made a lot of noise about the kid deputy who had bungled a job and caused a man to get shot. Jim-Bob had backed off a little. It had looked as if the only solution was to pistol-whip the man, and he didn't want to do that. Little as one might think about it, a heavy gunbarrel could brain a man. But Mont Naylor had shown up in time. With that quiet, deadly way he had when he meant business, he just looked the cowboy straight in the eye, disarmed him and marched him off to jail. He hadn't said a word to Jim-Bob about it.

Now, with Jim-Bob standing by, Mont unlocked the cell door. "You can come on out now, if you're ready to pay for the damage down at Francisco's."

The cowboy didn't look nearly so salty today. Sheepishly he counted out the fifteen dollars Mont asked him for. "It's that tequila," he apologized. "I go out of my fool head on that stuff, and I ought to know better than drink it. I'm sorry it happened, Mont."

Mont nodded patiently, but his voice was firm. "Just be glad it was a deputy like Jim-Bob. One like Chum Lawton would've beaten half your brains out with a gunbarrel."

The cowboy turned to Jim-Bob. "I said some things last night that I didn't mean. Forget them, will you, kid?"

Jim-Bob said, "Sure." But he didn't fail to catch that last word. *Kid!*

After the cowboy was gone, Jim-Bob hung his head. "I reckon they all feel about me the way he did last night — that I'm just a dumb kid who oughtn't to be wearin' this badge at-all."

For the first time since the shooting at Jace Dunnigan's, Mont Naylor looked directly at Jim-Bob. "Son, I won't lie to you; there's some talk goin' around. But I'll tell you what I told John Trumpett after the funeral this mornin'. You're only young, not dumb. What you did was from lack of experience mostly. Give you time, and you'll be all right."

Jim-Bob stared hopefully. "You're givin' me another chance?"

Mont nodded. "Never was any question about it. Only, you better watch yourself a while. Step like you was walkin' on eggs. Someday you'll get a chance to prove yourself. Just don't let folks squeeze you out of this job before that chance comes."

Jim-Bob's throat was tight. "You don't know how much this means to me, Mont. I always remember Dad, and the way he wore that star. The only thing I've ever wanted was to be able to wear it half as good as he did."

Mont smiled. "You will, son, you will. Now I think it might be smart to get you out of sight a day or two. Out of sight, out of mind, they say. How about runnin' a little errand for me, a personal errand?"

"Sure."

"I got a little bunch of broncs over at the corral — swapped for them the other day. I'd be much obliged if you'd take them out to George Thorn's ranch in the mornin'. He's goin' to break them for me."

Jim-Bob nodded happily. "I'd be tickled, Mont." A sudden thought dampened his enthusiasm a little. "Say, Mont, Chum Lawton's

39

workin' out there, ridin' broncs for Thorn. He doesn't like me much."

Mont frowned. "I know that, but I still need you to go. You just keep an eye out for Chum, you hear me? Don't let him sucker you into a fight. He'll jump at the chance to make you look bad, because he knows the ice is a little thin under your feet right now. You watch him, Jim-Bob and whatever you do, don't fight with him."

It was good to get away from town and the feeling that people were watching him. Jim-Bob left Mont's corrals at daylight, angling the horses northward up the wagon road toward Grafton. The Thorn outfit lay roughly halfway between the two towns, a little to the east of the road along the dry fork of Paint Horse Creek.

The red dog Ranger followed a while, chasing rabbits and barking at the broncs whenever they strayed off the road. Finally, when he figured Ranger had gone as far as he safely could without getting sore-footed, Jim-Bob ordered him to return home. It took twice to get the job done. Jim-Bob turned in the saddle and watched the dog trod disconsolately back along the wagon road toward Swallowfork, tail tucked under a little. Presently a jackrabbit bobbed up, and Ranger was off after him, his hurt feelings forgotten in the joy of the wild chase.

Jim-Bob grinned and gave his attention once more to the horses. They were young broncs and acted like a bunch of kids would act, running at first, kicking and biting and playing in the cool air of the early morning. And like kids, they tired of it after a while. They settled down to a long, steady trot. Each horse found his own place and more or less stayed in it.

Jim-Bob trailed along behind them and let them have their heads so long as none of them tried to pull away. For a while he felt like a cowboy again, jog-trotting across the wide mesquite flat in the dusty wake of the broncs. He had long since decided there was no future in cowboying if a man wanted to build something that would really be his own. But as a way of life, if he was willing to work for someone else, it carried a lot of satisfaction.

About four miles out of town, along the Grafton road, lay the Kendrick ranch. In size it was second only to Walter Chapman's C Bar. Where everything on the Chapman outfit was built for stout rather than for looks, and everything had a purpose or wasn't tolerated, the Kendrick outfit was something of a showpiece. A big white two-storey house stood out on the open flat, rising up beyond the straight lines of planted trees like a toothpick out of a pie. The paling fences gleamed with white paint, and even the barn was white.

As a common working cowhand, Jim-Bob had never been invited up to the big house. But cow country rumor had it that the family ate its meals on a large white linen tablecloth, with a young Mexican maid standing there to keep the coffee cups full and carry off the dishes as quickly as they were used. They said Mrs. Kendrick never had to cook or wash her own dishes. The story was told that once her own cook fell suddenly ill, and Mrs. Kendrick had gone without food for a whole day rather than eat anything that came from the cowboys' cookshack. There was supposed to be a white porcelain bathtub in the house, too. Old Ox Quisenhunt, the freighter, once told Jim-Bob he had seen it himself, had hauled it down from the railroad at Grafton behind a "grass freight" team of oxen.

But naturally the prettiest thing about the place was Tina Kendrick, the rancher's daughter. When Ox had told Jim-Bob about the bathtub, Jim-Bob had immediately pictured Tina sitting in it. The idea brought a blush and a quick surge of shame. Somehow now, every time he saw Tina Kendrick he thought about that bathtub, and about her sitting in it. It was a naughty thought but a pleasant one, and that faint tugging of guilt was never enough to banish it from mind.

Tina Kendrick fitted with a big white ranch-house, white tablecloths — and yes, even with a white porcelain bathtub. She was as pretty as a china doll. Just looking at her around the dances was enough to take most men's breath away. To a working cowhand like Jim-Bob, she had always seemed like a beautiful prize, far away and unobtainable. Small wonder it shook him when she had paid so much attention to him at Sothern's barn dance the other night. It was like a broke and hungry cowboy suddenly discovering a hundred dollars in his pocket.

Coming upon the white buildings of the Kendrick ranch with his string of broncs, Jim-Bob didn't really mean to stop. But he found himself angling the horses up the dusty road to the house before he realized what he was doing. He felt suddenly foolish. He had no real business here. Now it was too late to turn the horses back, for chances were he had already been seen. And what was it Mont Naylor had told him one day? "Once you've started down the hill, it's safer to go ahead than try to turn around and go back."

He saw an open corral gate near the barn and eased the horses through it. Jim-Bob stepped down inside the corral and shut the gate behind them, wondering what in thunder to do next. In an adjacent pen, nearest the barn, he saw an old pensioner shoeing a horse in the cool of the morning. The aging cowpuncher finished up. He dropped the horse's forefoot and slipped the rope off its neck, turning the animal loose. He was too busy to notice Jim-Bob.

"Button," he called to someone in the barn, "Button, you git yourself out here where you belong."

In a moment a cowhand a couple of years younger than Jim-Bob stepped out of the barn. He looked like a cat caught with its paw in the birdcage. The old man was bawling him out. "The boss left you here to help me with these horses, not to be lollygaggin' in the barn with his daughter. Now you pick up that rope and go catch me another horse."

Tina Kendrick appeared in the doorway of the barn. As the young ranch hand hurried off, building a loop in his rope, the old man testily turned to her. "Your daddy won't like it, you down here at the barn makin' fools of these kid cowboys. Now why don't you git yourself back up to the big house where you belong?"

Tina Kendrick smiled and tickled the old man under the chin. She let her slender fingers run through his short gray beard. "Now Papa John, you don't mean to lift your voice to little old Tina that way."

The old man said sharply, "You can wrap the rest of the men around your little finger, but I'm too old to bend thataway. I've known your tricks ever since you were a little girl." His voice softened, though. She had him, just like she did the rest.

Tina's eyes lifted and found Jim-Bob, coming through the gate afoot. "Papa John, we've got company."

The old-timer turned and glared. "Another one. It ain't enough you got all the cowboys on *this* place tongue-tied. Now you got to go and bring them in from someplace else."

Jim-Bob hastened to explain. "I just stopped in to water my horses. I figured they were gettin' a little dry . . ."

The old man snorted. "Only four miles from

town, and this early in the mornin'? They wouldn't drink if you kicked them off in the river."

The young cowboy led up another horse. He was eyeing Jim-Bob suspiciously. Papa John caught the look and sniffed. "Nothin' makes me tireder than to hear some old fool wishin' he was a kid again. Believe me, I'm glad I got all that foolishness far behind me." He turned away from Jim-Bob and began petting the horse, easing his hand down the hind leg so he could pick up the foot.

Smiling, Tina walked up to Jim-Bob, her skirts swinging just a little. She had that kind of walk. She stopped a full pace away, putting her hands behind her and rocking back on her heels a little. She looked him full in the eyes a moment, her own eyes dancing. "What brings you all the way out here?"

Jim-Bob remembered his hat and took it off. "Well, I was just drivin' these broncs out to the Thorn ranch, and I saw your place, and — well, it's like I said, I wanted to water the horses."

The pen where Jim-Bob had turned the broncs had no water in it.

"I know better than that," she smiled. "You came by to see me."

He reddened. "I hope you don't mind."

"Of course I don't mind. Why, I was just thinking about you when you rode up. Isn't that a coincidence?"

Papa John snorted again.

Jim-Bob just nodded, glancing at her, then looking shyly away as an electric thrill worked all the way down to his toes. "It sure is."

Tina caught his arm and said, "Let's go up to the house and see if there's some coffee and cake left. You do like coffee and cake, don't you?"

He would have eaten coffee grounds and raw dough if Tina Kendrick had been serving them.

Tina looked back at the young cowboy who stood beside Papa John. "Willy, would you mind taking Mr. McClain's horses down and watering them in the big trough?"

The young man nodded. "Sure, Miss Tina. I'll be glad to do it." But the look that stabbed at Jim-Bob showed he had rather take the deputy down to the trough and throw him in it.

The big house was even more sumptuous than Jim-Bob had imagined. Lace curtains, fine mahogany furniture, linen tablecloth. He was afraid to walk on the carpets with his high-heeled boots and spurs, and he started to skirt all the way around them. Tina caught his arm and led him across.

"Silly," she teased, "this is all very plain. You can't hurt it."

He met Tina's mother, and he got an uneasy impression she disliked him right off. He decided this was a foolish notion. How could she dislike somebody she hadn't had time to get to know? Just the same, Jim-Bob sat thoroughly awed, afraid to touch anything because it all looked so fragile. He ate cake and sipped weak coffee in delightful misery with Tina, and felt as out of place as a bronc in a boarding school.

A most disrespectful thought crept unbidden into his mind. He wondered where they kept the bathtub. He tried to shut the thought out, but it clung stubbornly while his face reddened. He caught Mrs. Kendrick staring severely at him. A panicky notion struck him that she might be reading his mind, Tina and soap bubbles and all. She *was* a cold-eyed old sister.

He was glad when Tina at last led him out the front door. They stood on the porch together. She frowned, but her eyes were soft and blue.

"Jim-Bob," she said, "I had to promise Chum Lawton I'd let him take me to the next dance. But I hope you'll be there to rescue me. There's not anyone in town I'd rather dance with than you."

Jim-Bob swallowed. "You just give me the high-sign, and I'll rescue you any time you want me to." He drew a circle with the toe of his boot. "I was hopin' maybe sometime I could take you to the dance myself. Then I wouldn't have to be rescuin' you from anybody."

Her voice was soft. "You just ask me sometime, Jim-Bob."

He walked down off the porch and looked back at her. She threw him a kiss and tore him to pieces inside.

Tina's mother stood watching, well back from the door. When Jim-Bob was gone, she said brittley, "Tina, come here."

The girl came inside, laughter dancing in her eyes.

"Tina, have you no pride? Must you forever be carrying on with men like that? I didn't bring you up to marry some common cowboy."

"Who said anything about marrying one of them, Mother?" Standing in the doorway, she watched Jim-Bob open the corral gate and string out his broncs. Her smile widened as she saw the cowboy Willy follow Jim-Bob out and stare after him.

Her mother said, "I heard about this McClain and Chum Lawton. I heard they almost fought over you at the dance. Disgraceful!"

Tina nodded. "They almost did. Perhaps another time."

"Tina!" Mrs. Kendrick gasped. "You mean you *want* them to fight over you?"

"Why not? Someday you'll marry me off to someone with a rich and dull future, someone like Dan Singleton. But I'll always be able to remember that I once had men fighting over me like two bulls over a heifer."

"Tina!" Mrs. Kendrick gasped again.

"Don't be so shocked, Mother. I'll bet you've got plenty of memories you wouldn't tell Dad about. Well, I'm going to have some memories, too, to keep me warm when I get old!"

It took a while for Jim-Bob to get settled. He rode with his head down, day-dreaming about Tina Kendrick. First thing he knew, the broncs were completely out of sight ahead of him. He touched spurs to his horse and eased into a lope to catch up.

With time, the mesquite flat stretched out behind him. The land roughened up, going hilly, with mesquite-timbered draws slashing down among the hills. The draw grass stood belly deep to a horse where cattle hadn't stocked it too heavily. Along its edges, he came across Mexican sheepherders drifting their wooly Merino bands on the shorter grass. Sheep would fatten where cows drew thin, yet sheep would starve in tall grass.

The broncs had left the main wagon road and veered east. That was all right with Jim-Bob. He had to leave it sometime anyway. The Thorn ranch lay to the east of the road. The broncs were feeling good. Reining up a moment, Jim-Bob could hear them ahead, breaking into a lope. He spurred the brown again. He almost lost his seat when a startled jackrabbit jumped up right under the horse's hoofs and caused the mount to shy violently to one side. Jim-Bob grabbed at the horn and pulled himself back into the saddle. The left stirrup flopped where his foot had slipped out of it. He was glad no one had been around to see him. It always rankled a cowboy to have someone see him fall off of a horse, or grab leather.

He followed the broncs' tracks up over the brow of a hill and dropped down on the other side, then reined up again. Ahead of him he

49

could see the broncs heading pell mell for a wide draw, where five hobbled horses stood with heads high, watching. He saw smoke curling lazily upward from a campfire, and men running out to catch their horses. For a moment it looked as if Jim-Bob's broncs were going to carry away those in the hobbles. But instead, they stopped running and began to mill around, nosing the other horses, getting acquainted.

By the time Jim-Bob reached the camp, there had been a brief kicking and biting fight between one of his broncs and another horse. The older horse put the young bronc in his proper place, and things settled down. The broncs began to graze on the thick green grass and to bite off the long strings of drying beans that hung down from the scattering of mesquite trees.

Satisfied that his broncs were under control, Jim-Bob reined toward the four men of the camp. One of them stood with a rifle in his hands. Another had a thumb hooked in his gun-belt, fingers touching the butt of the six-shooter on his hip.

All of a sudden Jim-Bob got a weird feeling about this camp. He wanted to keep right on going, but he knew he had to cut the broncs out from among the hobbled horses. Mont Naylor had told him: "You ever find yourself in a ticklish spot, you just go right on as if you hadn't expected anything else. Don't ever look behind you or start backin' up. Just keep your eyes open and your hardware handy."

Jim-Bob pulled his horse up thirty feet from the campfire. He had let his hand ease down to where he could almost touch his gun, but he hoped the men hadn't noticed it. He tried to keep his face and his voice calm.

"Howdy."

They looked him over good, no friendliness in their eyes at first. Jim-Bob wished he'd watched the broncs a little closer, wished they hadn't picked this spot to drop down into the draw.

Finally one of the men smiled. "Howdy, kid. Git down, and we'll have dinner directly."

Jim-Bob said, "I didn't figure on runnin' into anybody. I was just takin' a bunch of broncs out to the Thorn outfit. I didn't go to let them run through your camp like they did."

The man shrugged. "No damage. Just surprised us a little, was all. The way they came lopin' in here, we thought it might be a — well, it might have been most anything. Horse thieves or somethin'." He looked about him. A somewhat younger man with much the same facial features still stood with rifle in his hand. "Buster," the man said, "put that thing up. You want this boy to think we're unfriendly?"

The one called Buster was frowning darkly. "Ain't we?"

"Put it up, Buster!"

Jim-Bob hesitated, then carefully swung down from the saddle. He followed the example Mont had set at Dunnigan's — got off with the horse between him and the men. Jim-Bob knew just

51

about everybody in this country, but these men were strangers to him, and not very friendly strangers at that.

"Don't mind Buster," the man said. "He's just a little ringy. He thought them broncs of yours was fixin' to run off our horses. He sure does hate to walk." He extended his hand. "I'm Dencil Jones. Buster's my brother."

Warily Jim-Bob shook his hand. The one who called himself Dencil Jones pointed a thumb toward the other pair of men. "That's Pony Sims, there with the bald head, and the other one we just call Hackberry."

Sims and Hackberry shook Jim-Bob's hand, but he could feel their eyes working him over questioningly. Buster Jones stayed back. He had dropped the rifle from its ready position, but he still held it slackly in his hand.

"Ridin' hell-bent into a man's camp like that," Buster Jones said darkly, "how were we to know you weren't tryin' to run our horses off?"

Jim-Bob shook his head. "You don't have to worry about me stealin' your horses. I'm Jim-Bob McClain, deputy for Sheriff Mont Naylor." He reached up and touched a finger to his badge. But he realized they must already have seen it. Something lay cold in the pit of his stomach, and for a moment he wished he'd had that badge in his pocket instead of out in the open that way.

Dencil Jones was pleasant now, but Jim-Bob thought he sensed an undertone of worry in the man's voice. "What's a deputy sheriff doin' way out here?"

Jim-Bob explained his errand. Dencil Jones seemed to believe him. But Buster Jones still scowled. He had gone back beyond the fire and hunkered down well away from the flames' heat. He had laid the rifle down within close reach.

Jim-Bob licked his lips, for they were still dry. He found it hard to take his eyes off Buster Jones, and Buster's rifle. "You fellers are a long ways from anyplace yourselves," he remarked, not wanting to ask them straight out.

Dencil nodded, noting how Jim-Bob watched his younger brother. "Don't worry about Buster," he said. "Like I told you, he's just a mite ringy. He don't trust nobody lately that wears a badge."

He poured black coffee into a tin cup and handed it to Jim-Bob, following it up with another cup that had a spoon and some sugar in it. "We just finished drivin' a bunch of cows up to the TP railroad for the Circle Dots down south. While we were in Grafton, Buster took on a little too much of that happy juice and like to've wrecked the place. We decided we'd best hole up out here in the brush a few days till things kind of blew over, then head on south. Buster saw your badge and naturally thought you'd come to get him, was all."

It sounded all right, but Jim-Bob couldn't swallow it, somehow. He tried to keep from showing his doubt. "I hadn't heard anything of it. If it happened in some other county, it's none of our lookout anyway."

Dencil glanced at his brother. "See there, Buster? Settle down now." To Jim-Bob he said, "I could tell you were a right kind of a law when I first saw you. Buster didn't mean no harm in Grafton. He's just a little too playful sometimes."

Jim-Bob nodded. "Sure, I savvy." But he didn't. All he knew for sure was that something was wrong here. But he found his nervousness easing.

Pleasantly Dencil Jones said, "Why don't you stay and eat dinner with us? We'll be fixin' it directly."

Jim-Bob believed Dencil sincerely meant it, although Buster still scowled. Normally it was about half a day's ride to the Thorn place from Swallowfork. But Jim-Bob had lost time around the Kendrick ranch. It was still a couple of hours to Thorn's, and his stomach was growling at him. Moreover, he was curious. "I don't reckon it'd hurt to stay," he said.

Squatting on his spurs in the tromped-down grass, he studied the Joneses. Remarkable how much the brothers resembled each other. Much more than did Tom and Dan Singleton. Dencil was the oldest, and the years had set deeper in the lines of his face than they had in Buster's. But a stranger might easily be confused by the two.

"Easy enough to tell that you two are

brothers," he remarked.

Dencil smiled. There was an easy-gowg quality about him that Buster didn't show. "I don't reckon we can help that."

Jim-Bob looked out toward the broncs to be sure they weren't straying. They were remaining well put, enjoying the good grass. He studied the Jones outfit's horses. Mont Naylor would give his eye teeth for horses like those. It was seldom you saw a group of cowboys so uniformly well mounted.

He said, "You couldn't have a better bunch of horses if every one of them was stolen."

Buster darkened a little. Jim-Bob spoke quickly, "I didn't mean anything by that. Just a manner of speakin'."

Dencil laughed, but somehow it was a strained sort of laugh. "A cowboy workin' for the other man never has a chance to accumulate much of the world's goods, Jim-Bob. I always figure he's at least entitled to own a good horse."

The one they called Hackberry did the cooking. He sliced venison from a quarter hanging up in a mesquite limb and started mixing dough in a flour sack. He punched a hole in the center of the flour with his fingers, then carefully worked it with his hands, adding salt and baking powder as he squeezed water and flour into dough. He had no Dutch ovens, for the men carried only what they could pack behind their saddles. He fried the bread in an open skillet.

Meanwhile, to pass the time, Jim-Bob sat in a

card game with Dencil and Pony Sims. Buster Jones didn't play. He walked off down the draw, looking at the horses. Every time Jim-Bob glanced that way, he found Buster staring at him.

An idea had been nagging at Jim-Bob. Maybe these men *were* horse thieves. There was no getting around the fact that these were mighty good horses for four drifting cowpunchers. Jim-Bob had noted that no two of the horses carried the same brand. He tried to figure out some of the brands, but none of them were familiar to him. He would remember them, though. They might bear a little checking.

When he got back to town, he thought, he'd tell Mont Naylor about these men. Maybe they'd prove out harmless. Then again. . . . Well, it would keep. Right now he had to get these horses out to Thorn's. Time enough in a couple of days to talk to Mont. It didn't look as if these men were fixing to go anywhere anyway.

He saddled up after dinner and prepared to gather his scattered broncs. Dencil Jones stepped out to shake hands with him. "Come back by," he invited. "We'll be around a while."

Even suspicious, Jim-Bob found himself liking this man. "I may do that."

He separated his broncs from the Jones horses and stretched them out again in a long trot. The hobbled horses wanted to follow. Jim-Bob had to push them back twice. The last time he looked, he could see that Buster Jones was still watching him.

Buster scowled as Jim-Bob left. He walked back to the campfire and picked up the rifle. Dencil said sharply, "Put it down, Buster."

Buster replied, "We're makin' a mistake, lettin' him ride off like this. We could still get him, and nobody would know."

"He'd be missed."

"Not before we finished the job we been figurin' on. Afterwards, it wouldn't matter."

Dencil Fox sternly shook his head. "I swear, Buster, I don't know what ails you sometimes. I do believe you just like to see the blood run. He's only a green kid. He can't hurt nothin'."

"Maybe he's green and maybe he ain't. I wasn't any older than him the time we took that bank in the Panhandle, and there wasn't anything green about me, remember? I still say we oughtn't to take the chance." He took a step forward, toward his horse.

Dencil reached down and yanked the rifle out of Buster's hands. "*I'm* runnin' this outfit, and I say there's not goin' to be any unnecessary killin'. You want us all to hang?"

"Let the wrong people go ridin' around free and we'll hang anyway."

Anger crackled in Dencil Fox's voice. "Any time you decide you don't like the way I run things, you can leave. But as long as you stay with us, I'm the big brother. You savvy?"

Buster tried angrily, but he couldn't meet

Dencil's blazing eyes. "Maybe someday I *will* leave," he said and abruptly turned away. He walked to where his saddle lay on the ground. He took a bottle out of a saddlebag and worked the cork out with his teeth.

"You better go easy on that stuff, too," Dencil prodded him.

Buster spat the cork out in the grass, showing that he didn't intend to put it back into the bottle. "You go to hell!" he said.

Chapter Three

George Thorn's ranch wasn't exactly a poverty outfit, but it wasn't enjoying any excess of prosperity, either. George was a long-time cowboy who had saved his money for years and invested it in mares. In time he had himself a sizable bunch of horses. His TX horses were used all over West Texas. George would sell them either broken or as broncs. Besides that, he would break other men's horses for them if they couldn't or didn't want to do it themselves. He would charge by the head, depending upon the degree of roughness the owner wanted ironed out.

But these days George had to pay someone else to do the really rough stuff. Oh, he could still handle them pretty smartly himself, once the sharp edges had been rubbed down a little. He could still ride a bucking horse better than Jim-Bob ever could, even with his gray hair and the way his shoulders were becoming stooped a little more each year. An old bronc stomper like George Thorn might be forced to slow down, but he was unlikely ever to quit so long as he could still get on one by himself or get somebody to leg him up.

"A new horse is just like a new woman," George often said. "You can't stand the curiosity. You've just got to see for yourself how they turn out."

The first thing a casual visitor might notice would be George's corrals. They were better than his house. Fact was, they had to be, or the broncs would tear them down. The posts were of good heart cedar, six to eight inches thick across the top, and sunk as deeply into the ground as a man would care to dig with a crowbar and a coffee-can scoop. The planks were of good strong pine, hauled down by wagon from the railroad at Grafton.

The planks in the house appeared to have been leftovers from the corrals. George Thorn had spent half his days out in the open, following a chuckwagon. It didn't take much of a house to look good to him now.

The hot afternoon sun was well along its descent when Jim-Bob put the broncs through the gate of an empty corral and stepped down in the dust to shut it behind them. Narrowing his eyes in the summer glare, he could see two men out a-horseback in the distance. Their horses were crow-hopping around, evidently broncs out of the corral for their first time under saddle. The men rode in circles, yanking the horses around, getting them used to the rough pull of the inch-thick hackamore reins. Every once in a while one of the horses would bog his head and take three or four jumps.

"Howdy, Jim-Bob," a girl's voice called pleasantly. "Come on over and I'll put you to work."

Jim-Bob saw Sue-Ellen Thorn working in the adjacent corral. She had three hackamored broncs tied along the fence. She was sacking out a fourth. Holding the single rein, she gently threw a saddle blanket upon the pony's fear-humped back, then pulled it off again and again, getting him used to the feel of it against his touchy hide. The bronc's left hind foot was tied up so he couldn't jump around or kick much.

"Easy now, be gentle," she was saying softly, constantly talking to the bronc as she moved around in the gray dust stirred up by restless hoofs.

Jim-Bob leaned against the fence and watched her between the planks. At eighteen, Sue-Ellen was a real cowgirl for you. Sue wore a broad-brimmed hat that had been made for a man. Her long brown hair was done up in braids and tied down to keep it from being windblown. A thick coat of dust lay on the brown blouse and the dark split riding skirt she wore. From a distance, one might mistake her for a man. Close up, he wouldn't. Even with this rig on, she was quite obviously a girl. Jim-Bob had seen her in a dress a few times, her hair combed out and prettied up with a curling iron. A man would hardly recognize her as being the same. But even when Jim-Bob saw her that way, he remembered her this way.

Sue-Ellen could be a nice-looking girl when

she dressed up. Not really pretty like Tina Kendrick though. Her face was sun-browned, and her hands were a little on the rough side. Tina's blue eyes always held a little of laughter, a little of mystery. They gave a man a vague feeling that she knew something he didn't. Sue-Ellen's large brown eyes looked at you frankly and honestly, and there wasn't any mystery about her. She had been brought up among men. She had the man's way of saying what came to mind, be it pleasant or not. If she didn't like you, you knew it right away and no foolishness about it. If she did like you, you knew that, too.

Maybe that was what made Jim-Bob shy away from her so much. She liked him, and she wasn't coy about it. It gave him an uneasy feeling, because the way he had always been taught, a girl was supposed to sit back and wait for the boy to make the first move. Or at least make him think it was his idea.

"Well," said Sue-Ellen, "did you come here to loaf? There's some more broncs over here need sackin' out."

Jim-Bob jerked loose his hornstring and took his rope down from his saddle. Walking into the corral where Sue-Ellen was, he said, "I'll help you. It's a man's job anyway."

That was like stepping on a sore toe. Sharply she said, "Oh, it is, is it?"

She let the bronc's hind foot down and retrieved her rope. She led him to the fence and tied him, then walked toward one of the other broncs. Stalked might be a better word. She was angry.

Jim-Bob realized she had declared herself into a contest with him. He pulled the slip knot of another hackamore rein and freed a second bronc from the fence. He saw Sue-Ellen build a small loop in her rope and drop it right in front of the bronc's hind foot, at the same time leading him up so he stepped in it. With a quick jerk of her wrist she took in the slack and pulled the horse's foot up. Doubling and redoubling the rope, she tied it around the bronc's neck. Quickly Jim-Bob moved to do likewise. But Sue-Ellen had her horse's foot tied up before he did. He flushed in vague resentment, letting a girl beat him this way. Corral was no place for a girl anyway.

He thought back to all the times he had ever seen Sue-Ellen, and it seemed she was always conspiring to make him uncomfortable. He remembered one day she had been visiting the C Bar chuckwagon with her father. Jim-Bob had missed two loops at a wormy calf. Sue-Ellen borrowed somebody's rope, rode out and dropped a loop over that calf's neck just as neatly as any other girl might make a hemstitch. The boys around the wagon had razzed Jim-Bob until he'd finally had to bloody one of their noses.

Then the other night at Sothern's barn. He had been trying to dance with Tina Kendrick, but every time he glanced around it seemed that Sue-Ellen's eyes were on him. She wanted him to dance with her, and she didn't make any secret about it. He knew Tina could tell it, and it made him uneasy. But he had never given Sue-Ellen the satisfaction of dancing with him. She ought to learn it was a woman's place to wait and be asked.

"What did you come out here for, anyhow?" she asked belligerently as she began to work the bronc with a saddle blanket.

"I brought out some of Mont's broncs for George to break."

"What's the matter, can't *you* do it?"

"That's not my job."

She said flatly, "From what I hear, you're not doin' too well as a deputy, either!"

Then, seeing the hurt in Jim-Bob's face, she was instantly apologetic. "I'm sorry. I had no business sayin' a thing like that. I didn't mean it."

"I reckon you did," he said tightly. "You were mad enough to say what you thought. And you're right, I did make a mess of things."

She dropped the saddle blanket to arm's length and faced Jim-Bob. "Anybody's goin' to make a mistake once in a while. Even as long as Dad has worked with these old broncs, he occasionally lets one of them get to him. You oughtn't to let it ride you that way."

Jim-Bob said nothing. Sue-Ellen walked over and touched his hand. "Please, Jim-Bob, forget I said anything. You just made me so mad there for a minute, that business about this bein' a job for a man. It really shouldn't bother me, I've heard it so much. It's just that Dad needed a boy to help him, and he never had one. So I've had to learn to be a cowboy for him."

Jim-Bob managed a smile. "Next thing you know, you women will be wantin' to vote!"

Eventually old George Thorn and Chum Lawton came in with their horses. It wasn't an easy ride. One would have to lead or drive the other a little way. Then, when his own bronc began acting up, the other did the leading and driving. By the time they finally got back to the corral, the pitch was pretty well gone from the broncs, at least for the day. But the animals still had a lot to learn before they would ever be cow ponies.

Old George waved his hand at Jim-Bob. The sudden movement almost caused him to lose his seat, for the bronc didn't especially approve it. Thorn had a certain easy grace when he was on horseback. The way he sat there, straight and proud, he looked like somebody sure enough. But when he stepped stiffly to the ground, he was something else again. George Thorn, with more broken bones than he could keep account of, hobbled around so awkwardly that it was almost painful to watch him. He had been thrown, stomped, rolled over on, walloped against fenceposts and tree trunks until it was a wonder he could get around at all. His right leg was bowed out of proportion to the left, result of a compound fracture's crooked healing. His left arm was drawn up stiffly. The knuckles of his big hands were knotted, and his right thumb had long ago been cut off between a slipping rope and an unyielding saddlehorn.

But he was one of that tough old bronc-stomper breed who loved horses in spite of all they'd ever done to him. He talked them and breathed them, and he mumbled about them in his sleep at night.

"Jim-Bob, *come le va?*" he spoke jovially, his friendly eyes squinted up with turkey-track wrinkles reaching back halfway to his ears.

"Fair enough, I reckon."

"Them the ponies old Mont was a-goin' to send out here?" Thorn asked. He peered at them through the fence a moment or two. When he turned away, he probably could have described every horse in there.

Chum Lawton's bronc was still humped up a little and giving him some trouble in getting out of the saddle. Jim-Bob wasn't much inclined to help him. Chum finally saw an opening and swung down quickly. The bronc pawed at him with one forefoot as Chum stepped clear. In anger Chum started to swing the knotted end of the hackamore rein at him.

George Thorn said quietly but firmly, "Easy now, Chum, it's just pony nature to want to git you. You got to see it his way." Then, uneasily, he added, "Chum, I think you and Jim-Bob know each other." He knew very well that they did, and he was watching them pretty close.

Chum was square-jawed and ruddy-faced. And his eyes always seemed to be angry at somebody. Chum didn't offer to shake hands, so Jim-Bob saw no need to force the issue. He just shoved his own hands in his pockets and returned Chum's glare.

Chum *was* an ornery-looking cuss, Jim-Bob thought. Just an uneducated cowboy who couldn't even talk English right and proper, and who wouldn't never be nothin' but a cowboy or a bronc stomper all his life. He wondered what Tina Kendrick could see in such a man.

George said, "I'd figured on takin' out a couple more broncs before we quit for supper. You're goin' to spend the night with us, aren't you, Jim-Bob?"

Jim-Bob nodded. "Figured on it. I'll take a bronc out with you."

Chum scowled. "You sure you can hang on one? I don't aim to spend all night chasin' after your saddle."

Jim-Bob's face heated. "You couldn't catch it noway, because you'd be afoot before I was."

George Thorn saw it was time to change the subject. He led his horse right in between the two young men and nonchalantly began unsaddling him. Chum and Jim-Bob both scrambled to get out of the way. "If you boys are goin' with me, you better pick you a couple and throw a hack on them."

It was turning dark by the time they got the

three broncs back into the corral, unsaddled them and led them out to stake them for the night. Sue-Ellen had taken the others out one by one and tied them around to big old freight-wagon wheels, loose stumps, and anything else heavy enough to be hard dragging but not quite solid enough to break a bronc's neck if he made a hard run against the rope. By the time the broncs had been staked out a few nights, they learned plenty of respect for the hackamore that rubbed all the hide off their noses.

Jim-Bob's right leg was sore. Chum had bucked his bronc into him a couple of times. Jim-Bob was certain he'd done it on purpose. He had tried to return the favor but had been able to get his own bronc to buck only once all the time they'd been out of the corral.

The three men walked into the house with their spurs a-jingle just as Sue-Ellen lighted a pair of kerosene lamps in the small kitchen. "Supper's on the table," she said. "You-all wash up."

Jim-Bob noted that she had changed to a cotton dress. It looked better on her than those outdoor clothes. This was more the way a girl was supposed to look, he thought. She had hot biscuits and real milk gravy and steak. And the coffee — it was the real thing. No disrespect, but that coffee Tina had served him this morning had been as weak as water. Maybe someday he would get a chance to teach Tina how to fix coffee.

"Sue-Ellen," Jim-Bob finally said when he was

able to stop eating for a minute. "I didn't have any idea you could cook like this."

She talked angry, but he couldn't tell whether she really was or not. "Any reason why you thought I couldn't?"

Watching his step, he replied cautiously, "No, I didn't say . . ."

"You didn't have to say it, it stood out all over your face. You didn't think I could do anything but handle broncs and rope cattle. Well, I can do that and cook too. I'll bet *you* can't."

"No, ma'am," he admitted quietly, "I sure can't."

This girl was making him about as nervous as Tina Kendrick did, but in a different way. He didn't mean to be setting her off like that all the time. What did she want to be so touchy for?"

George came to Jim-Bob's aid. "Well, to be honest about it, she doesn't cook like this every day, Jim-Bob. Only when she's got company she likes. If you'd come here a little oftener, I might get a little tallow on my ribs."

Chum stared malevolently at Jim-Bob. "You say you can't cook, and you can't ride. I just been wonderin' what you *can* do, Jim-Bob. They tell me you couldn't even keep out of the way of a stinkin' old cow thief."

Jim-Bob stiffened.

George Thorn said quickly, "Cut it out, Chum. Jim-Bob does the best he can."

Chum said, "That ain't much."

Jim-Bob stood up, his chair scraping back

across the floor. "Now you listen here . . ." Then he remembered what Mont Naylor had told him. No matter what he did, he wasn't to let Chum Lawton sucker him into a fight. He sat back down.

But Chum was standing up. "Listen to what?" he challenged. "Seems to me like you got quiet in an awful hurry."

Jim-Bob looked down at his plate, his face flaring. He poked a tender piece of steak into his mouth. But now it was tasteless.

"I can't fight you, Chum."

"Or *won't*."

George Thorn quietly but firmly slapped the palm of his huge hand down on the table. "You two young roosters just settle down there. I can whip the both of you if I have to. There'll be no fightin' in my house."

Jim-Bob glanced up at Sue-Ellen and saw the question in her brown eyes. She was probably thinking he was scared of Chum Lawton. That brought him a flush of shame. He had rather be accused of stealing sheep.

"I made a promise to Mont Naylor," Jim-Bob said. "I told him I wouldn't fight with Chum, no matter what happened."

He realized suddenly that admitting this was the dumbest stunt he'd pulled all day. Now, knowing Jim-Bob wouldn't fight, Chum would needle him without mercy. Jim-Bob could see that idea working around in Chum's eyes. The way the story would get told, it would make

Jim-Bob out a coward.

After supper they sat on the front porch, in the darkness, enjoying the cool of the evening after such a hot day. George Thorn made some effort to start conversation, but it raveled out to nothing, and he finally fell quiet. Jim-Bob sat on one end of the little porch, Chum on the other. Eventually Chum got up and walked out to the shack where he slept.

George cleared his throat and knocked burned tobacco out of his strong pipe. "I'd figured on Chum sharin' the shack with you, but I don't reckon we'd any of us get any sleep tonight. Barn suit you all right?"

"I was going to suggest it myself," Jim-Bob said.

George lent him a pair of blankets, and Jim-Bob walked out to the barn. Presently he decided it was too hot in there, so he carried them outside and spread them in a corral on the off side away from the house. He lay awake a long time, dreaming how good it would be to arrest Chum Lawton stealing horses or smashing up a saloon. He didn't know when he finally went to sleep, but it was awfully late.

Awakening slowly, he opened one eye and saw that daylight was coming on. He became aware of noise. Sleepyheaded, he raised up on one elbow to see where it was coming from. Suddenly he was wide awake and on his feet. A dozen horses were spilling through the corral gate on the run, headed straight for Jim-Bob. He grabbed at the blankets and sprinted barefooted for the barn, the blankets wadded under his arm. Jim-Bob's shoulder slammed hard against the barn wall, and he turned to see the horses trample across the clothes he'd dropped on the ground. One of his boots went sailing and came down in a shower of sand.

Chum Lawton rode his horse through the gate and drew up, his eyes laughing. "Oh, howdy, Jim-Bob," he spoke with sarcasm. "You up already?"

Anger hit Jim-Bob like a fist, and he started across the corral toward Chum before he thought better of it and stopped. He picked up his boots, his pants and his shirt. It took a minute to find his hat, trampled out of shape and half buried in the sandy corral. He slapped the clothes against the barn to beat the dirt out of them before he put them on over his long underwear. There was a ten inch rip right down the back of the shirt.

Chum said, "It could have been worse. You could have had it on."

"One of these days, Chum," Jim-Bob breathed. "One of these days . . ."

Chum laughed, unsaddled his horse and walked to the house for breakfast.

When Jim-Bob got there, George Thorn stared in surprise at his rumpled, dirty clothes. "You look like you'd been run over by wild horses!"

Jim-Bob glanced sharply at Chum Lawton.

"You might say I didn't miss it far."

Chum was keeping his mouth straight, but his eyes were laughing. "Town life's spoilt him. He's got to where he sleeps half the mornin'."

The significance of all this somehow escaped George, but he could tell there had been something between the two young men. He didn't pry.

Chum ate silently a while. Then, "How much they payin' you, Jim-Bob?"

Jim-Bob tried to ignore him, but he couldn't. "None of your business."

Chum shrugged. "Just askin'. Seems to me like with a kid in the office, the county ought to just be payin' a kid price. Save some tax money."

"Tax money never seemed to worry you when you had the job, Chum. They tell me you ruined all the horses the county furnished for you, and Mont finally had to make you furnish your own."

Chum grunted. "Yeah, I been wonderin' about that. I been wonderin' if Mont didn't go ahead and charge the county for horses I didn't use. After all, he's in the horse business."

Jim-Bob dropped his fork. He could swallow an insult to himself. But Chum was treading on holy ground when he began to libel Mont Naylor.

"Mont's never taken anything that didn't belong to him," Jim-Bob hotly declared. Chum studied him keenly, evidently sensing he had found the nerve that was the touchiest.

Chum asked, "Is that a fact? Can you swear he's never stole anything from the taxpayers?"

"You're lyin', Chum. You're eggin' me on because you know I promised Mont I wouldn't fight you."

Chum glanced at George and Sue-Ellen to be sure they were getting all this. Sue-Ellen was watching Jim-Bob, dismay in her eyes. George said quietly, "Let him alone, Chum. He doesn't want to fight you."

Confidently Chum said, "Sure he don't. Maybe he's gettin' into that county money himself. I been wonderin' why he was so anxious to steal my job."

"I didn't steal your job. You'd already lost it before Mont ever came to me."

"But you'd been finaglin' around to get it. And it seems to me Mont was all-fired glad to give it to you. Maybe you got a deal of some kind worked out between you."

Jim-Bob clenched his fists futilely beneath the table. "You're gettin' way out on a limb, Chum."

Jim-Bob saw how Sue-Ellen was staring at him, and he looked quickly away. She was probably thinking he had no spine at all to sit here and endure this, promise or no promise.

Chum kept shoving the knife a little deeper. "Sheriffin' don't pay any big money, and it's been a puzzle to me why a man like Mont would hang onto it if he wasn't gettin' something extra on the side." A glitter of malice worked into his eyes. "Maybe Mont wasn't the first one. Maybe your old daddy set the pattern, because he had it a long time himself."

Jim-Bob jumped to his feet and went around the table in three long, determined strides. Chum was caught off guard a second or two, for he hadn't really expected Jim-Bob to fight. He was standing up and pushing his chair back when Jim-Bob hit him. He tumbled backward over the chair and hit the board floor with a thump.

George Thorn grabbed Jim-Bob's arm. "You don't need to do this for us, Jim-Bob. We know why you sat there and let him talk."

"I'm goin' to do this for *me*," Jim-Bob flamed. "Get up from there, Chum."

George said, "You made a promise to Mont, Jim-Bob. He had good reason to ask it of you. But if you're goin' to break it, then do it outside. I didn't build this house to stand up for a fist fight."

Chum pushed to his feet, gingerly fingering his nose that hadn't quite straightened out yet. It was beginning to bleed a little. "Suits me fine," he said. "Outside."

Jim-Bob walked out first. He paused on the bottom step to see if Chum was coming. Right behind him, Chum gave Jim-Bob a shove that caught him off balance and sent him sprawling into the broom-swept yard. As he got up, Chum was waiting for him. Chum caught him a hard blow that sent him staggering back.

Sue-Ellen stepped out onto the porch, but George gave her a quick nod of his chin. "Back into the house, Sue-Ellen. A thing like this isn't for girls to watch."

They fought around the front yard like two young bulls, slamming their bodies up against one another, rolling on the ground, grunting and groaning, hard fists driving. First one had the upper hand, then the other. Both men were bloody and bruised, their clothes torn and dirty. But eventually it began to work Jim-Bob's way. Ranch work had made him lean and tough. Chum had never worked particularly hard at anything. Jim-Bob was moving slowly now, but he still had some strength left. His breathing was labored but steady, while Chum was gasping for breath. Finally Jim-Bob was sitting up on Chum's chest, his knees pinning Chum's arms to the ground. Jim-Bob had Chum by the hair, lifting his head up and drumming it against the earth.

Breathing hard, Jim-Bob demanded. "Say it! Say you lied!"

Chum's bloody face twisted in pain, but he still cursed and squirmed under Jim-Bob's weight. Jim-Bob hammered his head some more.

"Admit it! It was all a lie!"

Chum alternately cursed and groaned, but finally he gave in. "All right, all right. It was a mistake."

"Mistake, nothin'," Jim-Bob said stubbornly. "You just flat lied! Tell George you lied!"

Desperately Chum admitted, "It was a lie."

Jim-Bob pushed to his feet and stepped back, watching while Chum turned over and got to his hands and knees. "You heard that, didn't you, George?"

Thorn nodded passively. "I heard it. None of it was ever goin' to be repeated in the first place." Shaking his head, he motioned Jim-Bob back toward the house. "You better wash up, then get goin'. We got broncs to ride here, and Chum's the only bronc rider I have. I can't afford to get him all crippled up fightin'."

Jim-Bob frowned. "How can you keep a man like that workin' here?"

"Bronc riders are hard to find. You got to take what you can get, because work's goin' out of style. Ten more years, there won't any of these young folks know what hard work is."

Jim-Bob heard Chum's boots on the ground behind him. Chum shouted, "Jim-Bob!" Jim-Bob turned just in time to catch a hard blow on the head. He dropped to his knees and it hit him again. Head drumming, he could hear a brief struggle and George Thorn's angry voice. A big piece of stovewood dropped to the ground beside him. He heard George say, "Chum, you get way from here and cool off before I take a notion to fire you!"

Next thing he knew, Sue-Ellen was bent over him with a washpan, carefully washing his face with a wet rag. Her lips were drawn tight. He thought she was angry with him.

"It wasn't my idea," he told her. "I didn't want to fight."

Tightly she said, "What'll people say when you show up in town like this? It won't matter what the real reason was, they'll say it all traced back to jealousy over that Tina Kendrick. For all I know, maybe that's what it really was."

"You believe that?"

"It doesn't matter what I believe. They'll say you're too irresponsible to wear that badge. They'll most likely take it away from you."

Jim-Bob gritted his teeth at the raw pain when she touched his left eye.

"Turnin' black," she told him. "You're a pretty sight."

Jim-Bob declared, "I'll be back to see Chum another day, when he can't get his hands on a chunk of stovewood. Then we'll see how pretty *he* is, with two front teeth gone!"

Chapter Four

Jim-Bob saddled up and reined his pony south again, toward town. He figured to get there by noon. Mont was likely to be disappointed. Jim-Bob knew Mont had hoped he'd stay at Thorn's a day or two and let things blow over a little in town. Jim-Bob had always gotten along fine with George, and he liked to fool around with horses. But Chum Lawton had been too much to take.

Jim-Bob rode along with fists clenched. He thought up two dozen ways he could cheerfully kill Chum Lawton, from rope-dragging him back and forth across a prickly-pear patch to drawing and quartering him between a bunch of wild broncs. They were all highly satisfactory but also illegal, so far as he could see. Bye and bye he managed to shove Chum Lawton from mind, and he thought of the Jones brothers, camped in the draw some distance above the Kendrick place. It occurred to Jim-Bob that it wouldn't hurt to have a look-see, just to be sure they were still around. Mont Naylor would more than likely be interested.

He smelled the mesquite smoke before he got in sight of the camp. Coming into the draw, he sensed that something was wrong. There was one less horse hobbled on the green grass today. Riding in, he could see three men in camp. He wondered where the fourth was.

The sound of his horse brought the men quickly to their feet. Dencil Jones turned, hand on his gun. He recognized Jim-Bob, and the sharp lines of his frowning face softened again. He raised his gun hand in greeting.

"Git down, git down and rest a spell." Somehow his face was not as cheerful as he had made his voice, though. Swinging down from the saddle, Jim-Bob led his horse closer to the camp's center and got a better look. Dencil's right eye was darkening. A bruise discolored one side of his face. The jaw was swelling a little. Knowing better, Jim-Bob asked innocently, "Horse throw you?"

Dencil shook his head. "A young bronc, you might say. Buster got the rings. He started drinkin' and took it in his head to go to town and raise a little cain. I tried to stop him, and I found out how old I was." Ruefully Dencil rubbed his jaw. "I used to could whip him. But I reckon a few years' difference is bound to show up eventually. Go yonder and pour you some coffee."

It must have been quite a fight. Flour and coffee and sugar were spilled out in the grass where the struggling men had fought and rolled over the camp goods. The coffee pot, now sitting on coals at the edge of the slumbering campfire, was bent so that the lid just balanced on it rather than fit the way it should. One of the coffee cups

80

looked as if a horse had stepped on it.

Dencil was watching Jim-Bob. A smile broke on his friendly face. "Looks like you must've run up against some kind of a bronc yourself." Jim-Bob grinned self-consciously and felt Pony Sims and Hackberry laughing with him. Dencil asked, "You whip him?"

Jim-Bob poured a little coffee into the cup, sloshed it around to wash the dirt out, then filled the cup to the top. "I did for a while. Then he got his hand on a chunk of stovewood. I lost."

Dencil's smile grew. He walked out to where a quarter of venison hung from a limb. He pulled out a butcher knife that was stuck in it and trimmed off two good slices of red meat. He brought one to Jim-Bob, then placed the other over his own darkening eye.

"Try that," he said. "They tell me it'll help take the black out."

Jim-Bob tried it. His eye ached. He couldn't tell that this made it better.

Dencil kept watching him, and finally he broke into a laugh. "We're a funny-lookin, pair, I do declare. A couple of black-eyed losers."

Jim-Bob didn't know that it was so funny, but he found himself laughing too, and he felt better for it. At the foot of a heavy-trunked mesquite lay a broken bottle. Dencil saw that Jim-Bob was looking at it. "That's what started it," he said, serious again. "I tried to tell him he'd had enough. I finally had to take it away from him and smash the bottle on that tree. He swarmed

81

over me like a hive of bees."

"Where did he go?"

"Swallowfork. To get a little drunker and maybe get in another fight. He'll come draggin' in tomorrow, maybe, like a whipped dog." Dencil frowned. "You look like a good boy to me, Jim-Bob. Don't you ever let that bottle make a fool out of you."

Dencil was still nursing a remnant of anger against Buster. Yet Jim-Bob could see worry deep in the tall man's eyes, too.

"Do me a favor, will you, Jim-Bob?" Dencil pressed. "When you get to town, look around for Buster. Sort of watch out for him. We'll give him a little time to work off his mad, then break up camp this afternoon and drift into town. Chances are we'll get him out of there before he does anything drastic. But just in case . . ." He shook his head. "I don't know what's come over him lately, he's just got plumb out of hand. I'm his brother, but I can't talk to him anymore."

Jim-Bob asked, "How long have you had the responsibility for him?"

A sadness lay in Dencil's eyes. "Since we was little kids, him about eight, me maybe twelve. Our ma and pa, they . . ." He broke off. "It don't matter about them." Looking at Jim-Bob, he asked, "You got a ma and pa, Jim-Bob?"

Jim-Bob shook his head. "Lost them a long time ago."

Dencil frowned. "It's a tough country thataway, throws a lot of boys out on their own long before their time. Some make out fine, and some . . .” He was silent a moment, his mind running back to times long past. “Somebody’s done a good job of raisin’ you, Jim-Bob. I wish I could have done better for Buster.”

Jim-Bob felt a tug of sympathy. There was no doubt in his mind that these men had heard the owl hoot, that somewhere somebody would probably give a plenty to get his hands on them. But these men were human, too, and Jim-Bob couldn’t help liking them. Especially Dencil. Dencil talked and acted like a half hundred cowboys Jim-Bob had known, common, friendly, easy-going.

“Sure, Dencil,” Jim-Bob promised. “I’ll keep an eye on Buster.”

Riding on toward Swallowfork, Jim-Bob thought of going by and visiting Tina Kendrick again. But he had run out of excuses. And he didn’t want her to see him all bruised up like this, his clothes torn. So he passed up the Kendrick ranch, although he kept glancing toward the white buildings as he rode by on the wagon trail.

The relentless gnawing of his stomach told him it was about noon as he rode into the main street of Swallowfork and turned toward Mont Naylor’s livery stable. Mont was sitting comfortably in the little bit of noon shade at the front end of the frame building, his cane chair leaned back against the wall. He had whittled a slab of pine boxwood down to a sliver.

"Didn't expect you back for a day or two," he said, surprise and disappointment in his voice. His disappointment grew plainer as he saw the darkened eye and the bruises on Jim-Bob's face. His lips pursed to form a whistle, but Jim-Bob never heard it. He was already too busy explaining.

"I couldn't help it, Mont. I know I promised you, but Chum was bound and determined. So I finally took him on."

Mont remained silent a moment, studiously whittling on what was left of his wood. "Whip him?"

"Nope. Got whipped."

Mont pondered a little, then shrugged. "One thing about it, you're honest. Most of them would've made some excuse about the other fellow gettin' hold of a club or somethin'."

Jim-Bob had been about to, but he swallowed it quickly. "I'm sorry."

The sheriff looked back to his whittling, his thoughts unreadable. "Can't be helped now. Better unsaddle your horse and give him some oats."

Jim-Bob led the animal through the big front door into the dim hay-dry interior. He silently unbuckled the latigo and slid the saddle off, swinging it up onto a nearby wooden rack. Tonight he would take it back out to his shack.

He heard Mont come up behind to stand and watch him. Mont said, "I know how you feel, son. I put you to a test, and you feel like you failed it. But maybe next time you won't. There's some hard lessons in this business." He put his hand on Jim-Bob's shoulder. "If you're goin' to be a lawman — and it appears you've made up your mind to do it — you've got to learn self-control. There'll be times you'd give your right arm just to get one poke at a man. But it's mighty often the wrong thing to do. You've got to forget yourself and remember what you stand for, wearin' the star. Let the other man be the one to lose his temper and come swingin'. You keep your wits and never let your temper get the best of your good judgment." Mont smiled. "I'll bet Chum looks as bad as you do. Go get your dinner, son."

Much relieved, Jim-Bob walked up to the bank and stood in the front door, looking around for Dan Singleton. He saw Dan hunched over a ledger in a teller's cage, running a pencil down a string of figures, his lips moving silently. Jim-Bob waited until Dan had finished totting up the sum, then asked, "How about dinner? It's time."

A big wooden clock with long pendulum began to strike twelve. The old banker True Farrell squinted up at it from his desk, then pulled a silver watch from his pocket as if he didn't believe it. He nodded then, satisfied, and smiled at Jim-Bob. "You'll never need a watch. You always know when it's time to eat." To Dan he said, "You buttons go ahead. I'll lock up."

Dan laid aside his ledger books and stood up,

stretching. "Got so wrapped up in those figures, I didn't even notice how hungry I was."

"Well, come on," said Jim-Bob. "*I* noticed." To Jim-Bob, figures in a book meant nothing. He could never understand how Dan so cheerfully accepted them as a challenge. A wild cow, now, which needed roping — that was something Jim-Bob could understand.

They stepped out onto the porch. In the daylight, Dan caught for the first time the dark marks on Jim-Bob's face. Seeing Dan's eyebrows lift, Jim-Bob headed off the question.

"Chum Lawton. I lost."

Laughter in his eyes, Dan said, "I wasn't goin' to ask."

"You'd have popped if I hadn't told you. Let's go down to Grammon's for a bowl of chili."

The weather-warped boardwalk rattled under the boots of men going home to eat. Jim-Bob stepped down to the ground and walked on the sand by preference, heading toward the little hole-in-the-wall where an old wagon cook named Grammon had set up a chili joint. Grammon's place specialized in Mexican-strong brown chili, and hot Java to cut the grease. It would never crowd the hotel dining room out of business, but it was a favorite with cowboys trying to save their money for essentials and spend as little as possible on such things as food. Five-cent chili stretched the summer wages and perhaps allowed a little extra tobacco or a spare pint. It wasn't the food that a man remembered when he got back to the ranch anyway.

Grammon was a middle-aged, heavy-set man with a deep voice which sounded as if he were talking down a barrel. He looked like he could wrestle a bull. He had cooked for years in the great open-range roundups that Jim-Bob could remember as a boy. Absolute master around the chuckwagon, Grammon ran his bluff on cowboys and ranch owners alike. Now that barbed wire fences had whittled the roundups down to size, Grammon maintained that the day of real men was past, and he had moved to town. He still ruled his chili joint as he had ruled his wagon. When it came to cleanliness and propriety, he could be as contrary as an old maid. Somebody was catching thunder as Jim-Bob and Dan walked in.

"You watch out there and don't slop that chili all over my clean floor," Grammon was telling a short, stocky cowboy. "Where do you think you're at, a chuckwagon?" When the cowboy started to lick the chili off his fingers, Grammon snorted and pitched him a washrag. "Some outfits, they'd make you eat out back."

The cowboy grinned at a tall man who sat beside him. "Slim, I always knew he was the ringiest wagon cook in the country, but I thought he'd be polite when he got to be a businessman and we was payin' customers."

The one called Slim smiled and said, "We haven't paid him yet," and went on eating his chili.

Grammon frowned at Jim-Bob and Dan, who were hunting a pair of counter stools that suited them. They were all alike. "When the bank and the law git to runnin' together, somebody better watch himself," he grunted "Did you come to close me out, lock me up, or eat?"

"Just hungry," Jim-Bob replied quickly. He had long ago learned the only defense against Grammon was a tongue as sharp as his own. "Got anything fit to eat?"

Grammon sniffed. "We just serve man-food in here, and I doubt that you buttons can take it." He dished them out some chili.

The stocky cowboy glanced at Jim-Bob's face. "Fall off of a horse?"

Jim-Bob looked him straight in the eye. "If I said yes, would you believe me?"

"Nope."

"Then there's no use me lyin' about it." And he dropped the subject.

The short one elbowed the tall one in the ribs, and both of them laughed. The pair were Harvey Mills and Slim Underhill, partners in a little ranch east of town. They had been young cowboys when Jim-Bob was a small boy. He still thought of them that way even though both were beginning to show some gray, and their eyes were getting the deep turkey tracks that came from squinting against the glaring Texas sun. Jim-Bob faintly remembered that Harvey had once been a deputy for his father, years ago.

People didn't pay much attention to Harvey

and Slim. The two had worked quietly for years, saving their money until they had enough to buy a little place of their own. They never spent much time or money around town. Theirs was just a greasy-sack outfit, maybe, but they were proud of it.

Jim-Bob always remembered John McClain saying Harvey Mills was one of the best deputies he'd ever had, although Harvey had decided he liked cow work better than being an officer.

"People like Harvey or Slim Underhill don't make as much noise as some," McClain had told his son. "But always remember that still waters are often the deepest. You ever need help, they're the kind that'll give you all they've got and never ask you any questions." Jim-Bob always thought of himself and Dan Singleton as being like Harvey and Slim. Working together, they'd amount to something someday.

Harvey Mills turned back to pestering old Grammon, who growled and enjoyed it. Jim-Bob and Dan ate silently a while. Finally Jim-Bob said, "Dan, what do you think of Tina Kendrick?"

Dan was reluctant to answer. "Really got you, has she?"

Jim-Bob nodded. "I went by there on my way out to Thorn's. Dan, she's the prettiest thing I've ever seen. You don't know what it is to see somethin' so pretty you've just got to have it."

Dan stared thoughtfully at a horse picture on Grammon's wall. "Maybe I do. I remember one time I wanted a paint pony. Neighbor outfit had it in its horse pasture. I used to ride over there and just sit and look at it over the fence. Tom told me it wasn't near the pony it looked to be, but I still had to have it. So one day Tom bought it. Spent two months' pay, the only real extravagance I ever remember in him. I was so happy I didn't touch the ground for a couple of days. I was just a little kid, and that was the prettiest pony . . ."

He sadly shook his head. "But you know somethin', Jim-Bob? It was just like Tom said. That pony wasn't much 'count for me. It never did make a cow horse, never was good for anything but show. I finally got so I didn't even want to look at it. I'd think how hard Tom had worked to earn that money, and I'd get sick inside. One day I told him to sell it, and he did. He didn't get all his money back, but he said the education was worth the difference. Maybe it was. I never have worried about paint ponies since."

Jim-Bob said, "You tryin' to tell me Tina is a paint pony?"

Dan shrugged. "Not necessarily. But she's cut out of a different pattern from us, Jim-Bob. Either she'd be tryin' to change you, or you'd be tryin' to change her. Do you think you could ever change?"

Troubled, Jim-Bob rattled the spoon in the empty chili bowl. Unbidden, a picture came to him of Tina eating chili in Grammon's joint, and he could see that it didn't fit. "I could *try* to change."

"And if you didn't make it?"

Jim-Bob hunted around for an answer but didn't find it. He wished he hadn't even brought up the question, and he felt a momentary stirring of anger against Dan. Dan Singleton sometimes had his older brother's way of bringing a fellow down to earth and jarring him hard. Maybe that was why he would make a good banker.

Hearing boots strike the floor, Jim-Bob looked up. In the front door stood Buster Jones. Jim-Bob was startled by the man's sudden appearance. He felt a twinge of conscience, for he had promised Dencil he would look around for Buster soon as he got to town. Other things had come up, and he had forgotten. He noted that Buster's face was flushed with drink, and his left eye was swollen. Dencil hadn't let him off scot free.

"Plenty of room inside, cowboy," Grammon said. "What'll you have?"

Buster started to answer. Then he saw Jim-Bob.

"Howdy, Buster," Jim-Bob said.

Buster stared in surprise, suddenly belligerent. He turned on his heel and stomped back out the door.

"Now what do you suppose made him act thataway?" Grammon asked, puzzled.

Jim-Bob said, "I think he was just born like that."

Dan frowned, trying to remember something. Then his eyes brightened. "I *thought* there was somethin' familiar about him. He came into the bank the other day. Had another man with him. They looked just alike. The other one did all the talkin', said they were brothers. This one watched me like he thought I was goin' to rob him."

In the bank? Alarm began to tingle in Jim-Bob. "What did they want?"

"Had a big bill. Wanted to change it and said they didn't want to try it at a store or saloon which might not be able to handle it."

Jim-Bob rubbed his jaw, his face creased. "They told me they'd never been in Swallowfork. They look the bank over pretty good?"

"I don't know — I guess so. What do you know about them?"

"Ran into them on my way up to Thorn's. They were restin' up after a cattle drive, they said. Names are Dencil and Buster Jones."

Dan said, "I'd have sworn they told me their name was Smith."

Jim-Bob stood up abruptly. "Somethin' queer about this whole deal, Dan. I think I'll go talk to Mont about it."

"Go ahead. I'll see you later."

"Sure," replied Jim-Bob. "See you later."

He tried the livery stable first. Mont wasn't there. It took some time before he finally caught up with the sheriff at the jail. Mont listened with interest while Jim-Bob told him about the Jones brothers. Or Smith, or whatever it was.

Eyes closed, Mont concentrated. "Dencil, Buster. Something about those names . . ."

He reached in a drawer of his big roll-top desk and took out a huge sheaf of dodgers. Putting on a pair of horn-rimmed spectacles, he thumbed through them slowly. At length he pulled one out and peered closely at it. "This is the one. I knew I'd seen it." He passed it over to Jim-Bob.

The name wasn't Jones, it was Fox. Dencil and Buster Fox. There was no picture on the dodger, but the descriphon left no doubt. Wanted up in the Panhandle for rustling cattle and running them across the New Mexico border. Wanted at Wichita Falls for attempted mail robbery. Wanted in Brown County for holding up a bank.

"Think they've got their eyes on this bank?" Jim-Bob asked anxiously, wishing now he had talked to Mont earlier.

"Could be. We better go talk to True Farrell."

Mont stuck the rest of the dodgers back in the desk and folded tho one about the Foxes. Jim-Bob felt a sharp pang of regret.

"It doesn't really surprise me none. I had just hoped . . . I liked Dencil right off. He treated me good, the kind of a feller you enjoy makin' a friend of."

Mont smiled, a thin smile of irony. "Time you're as old as I am, Jim-Bob, you won't take everybody at face value. Some of the nicest people I ever knew were crooks." Jim-Bob gave

93

him a questioning look at that, and Mont said, "I know it sounds funny, but it's so. Many an old boy who's good at heart slips off the track someway. Maybe he doesn't intend to at first, but each time it gets a little easier to do it again. Finally he's so far gone that there's no way to ever pull back." He shook his gray head. "I can't help but feel sorry for a man like that. Maybe there was a lot that was good about hirn, but he's wasted it. It's the waste that's so pitiful."

Mont took his six-shooter and gunbelt down from a hook on the wall where they hung most of the time. Around town, he seldom ever put them on. "Let's go, Jim-Bob."

Jim-Bob was at the door when he heard the shot. For a second he froze, his face draining cold. He sensed immediately where the shot had come from. He struggled for voice. "The bank!" he exclaimed.

He leaped completely over the steps, falling to one knee as he hit the ground. He faltered, got his balance, and headed for the bank in a hard run. Mont followed, but he was too far along in years to keep up with Jim-Bob.

Heads poked out of doors. Alarm whipped up the street as people saw the sheriff and deputy running. Other men dropped what they were doing and followed along.

Old True Farrell groped his way out of the bank's open door and grabbed onto a porch post.

"Doctor!" he shouted. "Get the doctor!"

Jim-Bob was fifty feet ahead of Mont Naylor when he reached True Farrell. He glanced at the old banker and saw he wasn't wounded. The excitement was probably too much for the man's heart. Jim-Bob rushed into the bank and halted abruptly. In a corner, a ranchwoman customer stood crying softly in the afterwash of terror. On the floor, in a spreading pool of his own blood, lay Dan Singleton!

Chapter Five

"Dan!" Jim-Bob choked. He dropped to one knee beside his friend. Dan gasped for breath. Jim-Bob touched the sticky crimson stain that inched outward from a hole in Dan's shirt pocket. Then he gripped the shock-cold hand.

"Easy, Dan. We'll take care of you." He dropped his chin and began to whisper a prayer. Dan coughed and tried again for breath.

"Hold on, old partner," Jim-Bob whispered, almost crying. "Doctor's on his way."

Dan Singleton tried, but there was no holding on. Jim-Bob felt the weak hand try to tighten on his own. Then Dan lay still. Jim-Bob began to sob.

Behind him, True Farrell was telling Mont Naylor about it. "We didn't notice the man till he was already in here. Came in the back door, I think. Had a gun in his hand. He forced Dan to give him all the loose cash there was around, then go into the vault. He pretty well cleaned us out. Dan said something to him, something angry. And this outlaw stood there cold as ice and put a bullet through Dan's heart. He went out the back door. He had a horse there, I'm sure."

Mont Naylor shook Jim-Bob's shoulder. "Run saddle us a couple of horses, son."

Numb from grief and shock, Jim-Bob stayed down on one knee. Mont shook him again, harder. Jim-Bob looked up angrily. "Leave me alone! Can't you see he's dead?"

Mont's voice went harsh. "He's dead, and there's nothing more you can do for him. Now you've got to remember you're a lawman. Go saddle us some horses, quick."

True Farrell said gently. "Go on, Jim-Bob. We'll take care of him."

Somehow Jim-Bob made himself get up. The gathering crowd made room for him as he moved blindly out the front door.

Old Leather Dryden, Mont's hostler, helped him saddle the horses. In a minute Mont came on to the livery barn, bringing with him four men he had lined up as a posse. There were the two partners, Slim Underhill and Harvey Mills. The chili man, big Grammon. And a broad-shouldered blacksmith. Other men clamored to go, but Mont had chosen his help. He wanted a few men of his choice, men he could depend on, rather than a big mob of men he might not be able to control. He was supposed to have them raise their right hands and swear an oath, but that was book stuff, and there wasn't time. These men knew what it was all about.

They picked up the tracks in the weedy alley behind the bank. The robber had had his horse tied back there, all right. He had headed north, up the wagon trail toward Grafton. There was no question as to who it was. True Farrell's description fit him to a T. Buster Fox!

Afoot, Mont Naylor might show his age. But on horseback, with a driving urgency upon him, he was as young as Jim-Bob. He spurred out in the lead, pushing hard. He had a big, heavy-boned sorrel, built to carry Mont's extra weight. The other men had to struggle to keep up.

Jim-Bob rode woodenly, the shock still heavy upon him. He was like a man asleep in the saddle, his reflexes keeping him on the horse because his mind was far away. He was thinking of Dan, of all the things they'd done together, all the plans they'd had — wild plans, some of them, but happy ones.

Dan Singleton, a fair-to-middling cowboy who was going to become the best cowtown banker in West Texas. Dan Singleton, the nearest to a brother that Jim-Bob had ever had. Jim-Bob was barely conscious of the hot wind rushing by his face, of the laboring of the running horse. But in a little while he began to sense that Mont had slowed down.

He heard Mont say loudly, "We've got no chance to catch up with him in a hurry now, and we can't afford to kill our horses."

It was when his horse heaved violently to one side to avoid collision with Mont's that Jim-Bob jerked himself up to reality. He found himself grabbing desperately at the saddlehorn to keep from going down under the hoofs of the horses behind him. It was like a splash of cold water in his face. Dan was dead, he told himself harshly. There was no way ever to change that. Jim-Bob could only hurt himself, grieving now when there was so much to do. There would be time later to think about Dan, a time when Jim-Bob could more readily accept the grim face of sudden death. The thing now was to catch up with Buster Fox.

After a while the white buildings of the Kendrick ranch began to bob up above the mesquite whenever the riders topped a rise. Mont hauled up short, so short that some of the others almost ran him down.

"There it goes," he said, pointing to fresh tracks on the ground. "He took off of the trail and out into the brush."

Harvey Mills swung down from the saddle for a close look. Jim-Bob remembered how his father had said Harvey was a first-rate tracker, that he must have some Indian in him. Harvey said, "Same horse, all right."

Mont pulled off the road and spurred out, following the tracks. Harvey Mills and Slim Underhill stayed close beside him now, for this might turn into a task for a tracker. But it wasn't. It soon became obvious where Buster Fox was headed.

"The Kendrick place," Mont said. "He's been runnin' his horse hard, and he'll be lookin' for a fresh one."

Jim-Bob's heart tightened up. Tina! What if

Tina was there? What if she somehow got in Buster's way? He felt his mouth go dry. Then he roweled his horse harder, moving out in front of Mont and Harvey and the others.

He was still a quarter mile from the place when he heard what he thought was a shot. A long moment later there came a couple or three more. Heart pounding wildly, Jim-Bob kept spurring, his lips flat against his teeth. He was well out in lead of the posse when he loped through the front gate of the corral and up toward the barn. He could see a couple of cowboys riding in excitedly from the other direction.

Then he heard a girl screaming inside the barn. Jim-Bob was on the ground and running before his horse ever came to a full stop. Gun in hand, he stumbled, got to his feet and ran to the barn. At the door he stopped, eyes wide in fear for Tina. What he saw in the barn was almost a duplicate of what he had seen in the bank. The old pensioner called Papa John was kneeling over a young cowboy who lay on his back on the dirt floor. This was the one called Willy. And he was dead.

Tina stood with her back to the wall, fists clenched against her terror-drained cheeks. She screamed wildly, out of her mind with fear. Running to her, Jim-Bob grabbed her arms. "Tina, Tina, are you hurt?" She seemed not to see or hear him. She just kept on screaming.

The other men rushed into the barn. Mont Naylor had the whole picture in one quick glance. To Papa John he said, "What happened?"

The old man shook his head. "I don't know exactly. I was up at the big house. . . ."

Jim-Bob couldn't hear for Tina's screaming. He shook her gently. "You're all right, Tina."

Papa John tried to go on, but Tina's screaming had unnerved him. Sternly Mont Naylor said, "Jim-Bob, try to quiet her down."

Suddenly Jim-Bob ran out of patience. He stepped back, hands still gripping her shoulders. Sure, she had a right to be scared, seeing something like this. But to go off the deep end that way. . . .

"Tina, snap out of it." He shook her, hard. "Stop it, I say."

Then, when she didn't, he slapped her. His hand left an angry red blotch on her face. Tina stopped screaming. But she stood as stiffly as before, her eyes fixed in terror, seeing nothing. Jim-Bob stepped back and looked away from her, ashamed. But not of himself. He was ashamed of Tina. He had slapped her, and when she came to her senses and realized it, she probably would never forgive him. But somehow, after all that had happened today, it just didn't seem to matter.

Papa John continued shakily. "I was at the big house rakin' the yard. I seen this feller come a-ridin' up to the barn in a big hurry. Willy here was supposed to be trimmin' the tails of some horses that had got tangled up in cockleburrs. I didn't know Tina was here. I've told her time and again not to go out to the barn where the cowboys was workin'."

Jim-Bob felt a cold chill. "She was out here with him?" He pointed his chin toward the dead cowboy. Papa John shook his head affirmatively.

"What for?" Jim-Bob demanded, then realized how silly it sounded.

The old man glanced at Tina, something of disgust in his eyes. He never answered Jim-Bob's question. "Feller must've wanted to change horses, and maybe Willy got in his way, I don't know. But I heard a shot and came a-runnin'. This feller threw his saddle on one of the horses and spurred out like the devil was chasin' him."

Mont turned to his posse men. "We better catch us some fresh horses, too. We been pushin' ours mighty hard."

One of the two cowboys who had come riding in from the other direction told Mont excitedly, "We didn't know what was goin' on. We met this feller ridin' out, and I reckon we got in his way a little. He took a shot at us. I happened to have my saddlegun along, so I gave one back. I was flustered and jammed the gun before I could get a second shot. But I'm pretty sure I hit the horse. I saw it stumble."

Mont said hopefully, "Then he won't get far. Forget about those fresh horses. We better ride."

Jim-Bob hesitated a moment, looking at Tina. He remembered what Dan had said about paint ponies, and he realized Dan knew what he was talking about. She was great for show.

Now there were eight of them after Buster Fox. The two Hendrick cowboys joined up. Mont no longer pushed so hard. He stayed in an easy lope, confident they would soon run the wounded horse down. They followed the tracks out across a broad mesquite flat, then down into the rockier breaks of a big draw that drained all the way to the Centralia. Here gullies spread like long crooked fingers from the rough hills above, where infrequent rains brought runoff water crashing down to eat away at the soil. Beyond, as the draw spread out, thorny mesquite brush grew like a jungle in the deep fine silt washed from the hills and the gullies. A few of the old cowmen like Mont Naylor were saying this was a result of overgrazing by cattle and sheep, that the grass was being grubbed off short and letting the soil work loose. But others said it wasn't so, that it just didn't rain as much as it used to, that the grass would come back as good as ever when seasonable times came again.

Occasionally they lost the tracks. Harvey Mills and Slim Underhill would get down and look around. It never took long for them to get straight.

"Horse is beginnin' to falter," Harvey said. "Here he went down. Fox got off and kicked him up again. But he won't get much more out of him, I'm a-thinkin'."

Mont Naylor frowned toward the thickening brush ahead. "Then he's down yonder someplace. He'll be lookin' for cover, and there's plenty of it in that brush."

They came to the Kendrick outfit's outside fence. It was four strands of barbed wire, still so new there was no rust on it. Harvey said, "He went across with his horse, right here."

Buster had knocked the staples out of a couple of fence posts on each side to loosen the wire. Then he had pushed the wires down and held them with his foot while he forced the horse to cross over. Jim-Bob stepped down and helped Harvey hold the wires to the ground so the other men could ride across. The wires sprang partway back up the posts as they turned them loose.

Worriedly Mont asked the Kendrick cowboy, "Did you notice what guns he was carryin'? Anything besides a six-shooter?"

"That's all I saw. But he might've had a saddle-gun."

Jim-Bob knew what was going on behind Mont's troubled eyes. It was bad enough to ride into the thick brush after a man who might be anywhere, holding a six-shooter. It was much worse to go after one who might be carrying a rifle.

Mont reined his horse around to face the other men. "You-all know what we're up against. With a rifle and a little luck, he could pick off half of us before we could find just where he's at. If there's any of you want to stay back, I won't think bad of you."

Jim-Bob edged his horse up to the sheriff's. "I'm with you, Mont."

So did Harvey and Slim. The Kendrick cowboys followed suit. There was a grimness in their eyes now. They'd had time to think about Willy lying there on the barn floor. At first, they had been too busy to let it dwell on their minds. The old cook Grammon and the blacksmith were the last. The blacksmith had a family. Seeing that the others were going, Grammon said gruffly, "We just as well go with them. We'd feel awful lonesome ridin' back to town all by ourselves."

The blacksmith's voice was nervous, but he forced a smile. "I reckon. Anyway, he'll shoot at you first because you're the biggest target." The two pulled their horses up to Mont's.

Appreciation was in Mont's eyes. "We better spread out then, and not give him too easy a target. If we find him, don't take unnecessary chances. He's killed two men today. We don't want any of us added to the list."

Grimly they spread out in the mesquite, a hundred feet or so between each man. Mont remained in the center as guide, following the tracks. His was by far the most dangerous position, and he accepted it without question. This was his job. He slipped his saddlegun out and touched heels to his horse's ribs, the gun across his lap.

Jim-Bob had no rifle. He drew the heavy old .44 and gripped it in a cold-sweaty hand. Moving into the thick brush, he could hardly make himself breathe. He held his breath until his chest began to ache. He rode slowly, weaving in and out among the thorny branches. His gaze flicked from bush to bush, from Mont Naylor on one side of him to Harvey Mills on the other. This gave Jim-Bob the same cold, sick feeling deep in his stomach that he got when beating the weeds with a stick for a rattlesnake he knew was there.

Looking off to one side, he let his horse carry him under a low limb. The thin green leaves raked his ear. He jerked around, gasping in surprise, swinging the six-shooter up. He came within a hair of pulling the trigger and firing into space. His heart was hammering. The blood roared in his ears. Another time, he would have gotten a big laugh out of it afterwards. But he doubted that this would ever be funny to him, not even when he looked back on it years from now.

It was silence here in the thicket. Not a trace of wind to rustle the leaves, not a bird singing, nothing but the quiet movement of horses through the brush, the swish of a green limb pushed aside, then springing back into place. The summer heat rose up thickly around Jim-Bob. It seemed to stifle him. He found his shirt half wet with sweat. His head itched beneath the leather sweatband in his hat. Sweat worked down into his eyes, burning them.

He came upon the horse then, Buster Fox's horse, standing with head drooped, blood trickling down the left foreleg. The horse was dying on its feet. Jim-Bob looked across at Mont

Naylor. Mont saw it and nodded.

"Shoot it, Jim-Bob," he said quietly, then passed the word down the line so the others would know what the shot was for.

Jim-Bob peeled off Fox's saddle and dropped it to the ground. He noted that there was a saddle scabbard, and it was empty. No question about it now. Buster Fox was in here afoot, hiding. And he had a rifle!

The horse stood unmoving as Jim-Bob slipped the bridle off its head. Jim-Bob took a firm grip on his bridle reins, not wanting his own horse to jerk away at the sound of the shot. He hesitated a moment, hating this. He had never shot a horse before. To him, it was almost like shooting another man. Then he pulled the trigger. The horse fell.

The spread-out posse moved again, slower now, knowing Fox could not be far away. Tension drawing tighter within him, Jim-Bob found himself wondering once why he had ever wanted to be a lawman in the first place. There was something infinitely unfair about this, good men having to ride along in the open this way, waiting for a killer to get first shot so that they might, if they lived, have a chance at the killer. Offering themselves up for sacrifice, as it were. Jim-Bob wondered if there were any job in the world that paid enough to justify that. But he knew what old John McClain would have said. With some men it is a sense of duty rather than any thought of pay. Men strong enough to stand up to the risk felt an obligation to their friends to use that strength in making the community safe. This sense of doing a worthwhile service was the job's own reward, a more satisfying one in its way than money could ever be.

A rattlesnake almost always gives a warning before he strikes. Buster Fox gave none. The high-pitched slap of his rifle racketed through the thicket. Jerking around, Jim-Bob saw Mont slump in the saddle.

Without thinking, Jim-Bob instantly spurred through the brush toward the sheriff. He was oblivious of the thorny branches that clawed him, ripping his shirt to ribbons, scratching his face and leaving tiny ribbons of blood on his cheek. He glimpsed Buster Fox crouched behind a mound of silt that had piled up in a many-pronged mesquite. Buster was levering another cartridge into the rifle. Jim-Bob fired at him once, a wild shot to make Buster dive for cover long enough for Jim-Bob to reach Mont and get him away.

He grabbed at Mont, got an arm around his waist at the same time he gripped Mont's bridle reins in his other hand. Spurring, he heard the rifle speak again. He felt the vicious snarl of the slug past his face.

Right ahead of him was a depression where bulls had been pawing sand. "Drop, Mont," Jim-Bob said urgently. He pulled away from the sheriff, turning his horse between Buster and Mont and letting Mont half fall to the ground.

The rifle cracked again. Buster Fox was not taking careful aim now. He was firing rapidly. It might be that he was as near panic as Jim-Bob.

Gun still in his hand, Jim-Bob swung to the ground and let the horses go. They ran away into the brush, frightened by the gunfire. Time enough to catch them later. Jim-Bob dropped to his belly in the sand and noted with satisfaction that he and Mont were lying on the off side of a small rise which would protect them from Buster's fire so long as they didn't raise up.

Mont's teeth were clenched in pain. Jim-Bob ripped away the bloody shirt and saw where the bullet had smashed into the shoulder. Jim-Bob used his handkerchief in a vain effort to stanch the bleeding. "Easy, Mont," he said quietly, "everything's goin' to be all right."

But he found his lips trembling and his voice trying to break. Mont was in agony, that was plain to see. The sheriff's kindly face was going pale. Jim-Bob touched Mont's forehead and felt it cold and clammy. It came to him then that Mont might die.

Strange how different things were when the time really came. Jim-Bob had often pictured a situation like this. He knew that a lawman lived always in jeopardy, that he might be called upon at any time to lay down his life. He had always assumed that when the time came he would simply brace himself bravely and take it.

But now it was here, and it was different. Here lay old Mont Naylor, one of the kindest men he'd ever known, bleeding and maybe dying in a bullhole deep in a mesquite thicket. Jim-Bob could hear the sheriff's labored breathing; felt the lawman's warm blood sticky on his hands. First Dan. Then Willy. Now Mont for a third victim of the ruthless killer who lay forted up only thirty or forty feet away, waiting his chance to make it four.

A black rage heaved up in Jim-Bob. Suddenly then, only one thing was important: to get Buster Fox. There was no time to consider fear. He glanced at the .44 again to be sure he hadn't gotten it clogged with sand. Then he was on his feet, rushing toward Buster Fox, firing as he ran.

Fox raised up and squeezed off a quick shot that tugged at Jim-Bob's sleeve, nothing more. Jim-Bob kept firing. He could see the bullets kicking up sand around Buster. Fox saw it too. One shot, two, three. Buster fought at his rifle. Then he stiffened in terror. Four.

Buster Fox screamed. "Don't shoot me! Don't shoot me!"

Five shots. That one kicked sand into Buster's eyes. Buster still held the rifle, could use it. But he stood helpless in panic, waiting for the sixth shot that wouldn't miss.

Jim-Bob stopped and aimed. At this range it was a certainty. Fox's chest was a broad target. Jim-Bob held the front sight on the third button of the dirty shirt. His finger tightened on the trigger.

Buster Fox sobbed, "No, kid, please!"

For a moment the rage was more than Jim-Bob could contain. It was so much that the gun wavered. He could not hold it true. Finally he lowered the gun. He tried to speak, but his throat was so tight he couldn't bring out a word. He motioned with the gunbarrel, and Buster Fox stepped out haltingly, his rifle falling to the ground, his hands lifting.

The posse men came running. They had been circling around behind Buster when Jim-Bob made his charge. They had had to scatter again to keep out of the way. Now they gathered around, covering Fox. Harvey Mills quickly checked Buster for a hideaway gun in his shirt, waistband or boottops. There was none.

Harvey said appreciatively, "Good goin', boy. If it had been me, I don't think I could have kept from killin' him."

Buster Fox went white. He dropped down in the sand and rubbed his sleeve over his eyes. Jim-Bob thought the outlaw was going to be sick. He gazed at him in hatred. Yet somehow he began to be glad he hadn't killed Buster. He was glad they were going to be able to take Buster to town, to make him pay properly for what he had done.

Jim-Bob got his voice back. "Mont's hard hit."

They walked back to where Mont lay. Jim-Bob knew the responsibility was his now, but he found no strength. He stood wavering, uncertain what to do. Harvey Mills understood, and he took over. There was a solid confidence about this rancher that commanded respect.

"Bullet's high, long way from the heart. Biggest danger is shock. Shock can kill a man even when the wound itself doesn't amount to much. We better get Mont to the Kendrick place as quick as we can. We can haul him on to town in a wagon."

The blacksmith brought up the question. "Where's the bank loot?"

In the excitement they had all forgotten about it. Jim-Bob tried to say something, but reaction had set in from the violent excitement. He found himself shaking, unable to talk.

Harvey demanded, "Where is it, Fox?"

Buster had regained some of his composure. He shook his head. "Go hunt it yourselves."

The men quickly scouted around where Fox had made his stand. They found no sign of the money.

"You didn't have time to hide it," Harvey said to Fox.

Buster just glared at him, not answering either way.

Harvey looked worriedly at Mont Naylor. "A couple of you fellers can stick around and look. We got to get started with Mont. You can catch up with us later."

They tied Buster Fox's hands. With his own horse dead, they put him on one of the Kendrick cowboys' horses. Then two cowboys stayed to search. Later, they would ride double.

Jim-Bob had to do something with his hands, had to get them busy. He started to reload the

112

old .44. He looked at it, then sagged.

"What's the matter, Jim-Bob?" Harvey asked. "You look sick."

Jim-Bob handed Harvey the gun, almost dropping it. "I forgot I'd shot that horse. There wasn't no sixth shot left in that gun!"

Chapter Six

The hot summer sun had lost its fury and was rapidly dipping into blood-red clouds on the skyline. The horsemen rode with their prisoner past the shack Jim-Bob had shared with Dan Singleton. Jim-Bob glanced once at the shack, thought of Dan, and looked quickly away. He wondered how he would be able to make himself return there. Usually the red dog Ranger would come out to greet him any time he happened to ride by the shack. He didn't see him now, and he wondered where the dog was.

Old Grammon and the blacksmith brought up the rear in a Kendrick wagon, hauling the wounded Mont Naylor to town. The word spread out before them like concentric rings that followed the dropping of a stone into still water. People stood silently on front porches and steps of their homes to watch the passing of the riders and wagon. Moving on down into town, the posse found a crowd gathered around the stores and saloons, the blacksmith shop and hotel. All eyes dwelt on this bank robber who had killed two men as thoughtlessly as other men might kill a rabbit. No one in the crowd had much to say. The quiet anger in their eyes spoke for them.

A disturbing thought began to creep into Jim-Bob's mind. Harvey Mills voiced it. "I got a prickly feelin' at the back of my neck. That jail-house may not be any place for honest men tonight."

Jim-Bob asked anxiously, "You think they'd lynch him?"

"Wouldn't surprise me any. I never saw a man deserved it any more than Buster Fox does."

"But he's a prisoner, Harvey. It's up to the law to hang him in its own due time."

Harvey shrugged. "What *is* the law, Jim-Bob? It's nothin' but a set of rules people have made up to help them live with each other. It's not sacred in itself. The people can change it. And these are people. If they decide to rush things up, is that much different from goin' by the law and takin' the long way around? The law does it for them if they don't do it for themselves. It winds up the same."

Jim-Bob had never thought of it in just that light. Fact of the matter, he had never thought about it much one way or the other. As he saw it, a law enforcement officer was not supposed to worry about the merits of the law. He was supposed to accept it as it was and see that it was carried out. He was a man who moved about his job with a quiet pride and an unshakable confidence, standing aloof from those who argued and wrangled. He simply saw his duty and did it. At least that was the way it was with John McClain and Mont Naylor. It was the way

Jim-Bob wanted to have it for himself.

"If we were goin' to kill him," he said firmly, "we ought to've done it out yonder when he still had a gun in his hand. Now he's our prisoner. We're duty-bound to protect him till they take him out and read papers over him and hang him legally."

Harvey had a grim smile. "Papers! Did I ever tell you why I quit bein' a deputy? It was those everlastin' papers. It seemed to me that lawyers and law officers in general worshipped those papers the way other folks worship God. A hungry man can go to the pen for stealin' a fat calf, but a land-grabber can steal half a county if he can find himself a crooked judge who'll give him a set of papers. And the sheriff will have to help him throw the widow off the land, like it or not."

Jim-Bob didn't know why, but Harvey's outlook needled him a little. He was a shade too young and inexperienced to understand all there was about it, and maybe when he got older he would turn cynical the way Harvey was. Right now, though, all he had to go on was what he had learned from Mont, and what he remembered of his father. The law had meant a great deal to them. Jim-Bob would not question it. By those standards, Harvey Mills was wrong.

Jim-Bob said, "I'll grant you that the law may be goin' to a great length to protect people like Buster Fox. But maybe at the same time it's protectin' the rest of us, too. Maybe there's no safe way to take a short cut on the law-breaker without takin' the rights away from the good people at the same time."

Harvey looked at him queerly. Finally he nodded. "I'll bet you learned that from your old daddy."

"I did."

Harvey said evenly, "You just go on believin' in the things John taught you. You'll never go wrong, boy."

Someone in the crowd called Jim-Bob's name. He pulled up, his gaze searching among the faces. Tom Singleton, dressed in black, stepped out into the sandy street. Dan Singleton's brother stopped and stood there, gaunt and straight. Hatred was a cold fire in his dark eyes. The sight of him sent a chill up Jim-Bob's neck. Jim-Bob moved his horse over beside Tom.

"This him, Jim-Bob?"

"It's him, Tom."

He sensed Tom's intention. The man's hand dropped and came up with a gun from the holster at his hip. Jim-Bob had no time to consider. Instinctively he threw himself out of the saddle and landed on top of the tall cowboy. They fell to the ground in a heap. Tom Singleton grunted in anger and tried to heave Jim-Bob's weight away. Struggling with him in the sand, Jim-Bob managed to get his hands on the gun. He hurled it away and saw Slim Underhill pick it up.

"Stop it, Tom," he said. "Stop it!"

Normally he wouldn't have lasted long with

Tom Singleton in a fair fight. But much of Tom's breath had been slammed out of him when he hit the ground. He gasped for air, the sweat breaking on his face as he tried to pitch Jim-Bob off.

"Let me go! He killed my brother!"

"Tom, stop it. You're not helpin' anything this way."

The struggle ended. Jim-Bob pulled away, panting, and stood up. Tom pushed onto his knees and rested there, trying to get his breath back. Jim-Bob said, "Tom, he's in my charge. I'm not goin' to let you have him."

Tom Singleton got to his feet. Angrily he dusted his black vest, his black trousers. Jim-Bob reached out, and Slim handed him Tom's gun. Jim-Bob unloaded it and started to give it to Tom, changed his mind and shoved it in his own waistband. He realized it was a futile gesture. If Tom wanted a gun, he wouldn't have any trouble getting one. From the looks of the men who watched, any one of them would have lent him a gun without hesitation.

Jim-Bob said evenly, "Tom, we been friends a long time, you and me. Dan and you were both like brothers to me. I'm as interested as you are in seein' that Buster Fox gets what's comin' to him. I don't want to see you in jail for murdering him. So stand off, Tom. Let things alone."

Tom Singleton's voice was like ice. "I'll get him, Jim-Bob! *You* stand off, because I'm goin' to get him!"

Jim-Bob heard a murmur of approval run through the crowd. He sensed that many were angry with him for stopping Tom. He spoke loudly, "You fellers better go on home and let things alone!"

To himself his voice sounded hollow. He knew it must sound that way to the others. It was just a kid talking. Who was going to listen to a kid? He got back on his horse and headed on toward the jail with Buster, Harvey and Slim.

Buster said, "Pretty fast work you did back there, keepin' that hombre from shootin' me."

Jim-Bob turned on him, eyes ablaze. "I want you to understand this right now, Buster, I don't care what happens to you. Personally I'd be tickled to death to see lightnin' strike you dead right here on the street. I didn't want to see Tom in jail for killin' you."

Hearing the rattle of chains, Jim-Bob looked back over his shoulder. Grammon and the blacksmith hauled the wagon team off to the right and pulled up in front of the doctor's small frame house. Some of the crowd followed along afoot, anxious about Mont Naylor. Jim-Bob waited a moment until sure the pair had plenty of help in lifting Mont out of the wagon. Then he moved on toward the jail.

He clanged the cell door shut on Buster Fox and turned away, not wanting even to look at him. In a second cell sat a man who had been arrested yesterday for fighting. Jim-Bob unlocked the door and swung it open. "You better clear out of here, Punch."

Punch looked surprised. "Mont say so?"

"Mont's not in shape to say anything. I think it's best that you go."

Punch stood up but cocked his head over doubtfully. "You guarantee you got the authority, boy? I'd like out, sure enough, but I don't want to get in no trouble over it. I got enough trouble now."

Jim-Bob's face warmed. "I'll take the responsibility. Now git!"

He slammed the door shut again and pitched the big key ring onto Mont's heavy desk. Harvey Mills and Slim Underhill had followed him into the jail. Harvey watched Punch leave and said, "Still havin' trouble provin' you've come of age, aren't you, Jim-Bob?"

Jim-Bob nodded and walked over to the front door. He leaned against the jamb and looked unhappily out into the street. "It was a mistake bringin' Buster in here. I can see that now. We ought to've taken him straight to Grafton or someplace as quick as we caught him."

Harvey said, "Hindsight's easy. It's foresight we all need more of."

Jim-Bob watched the street. He watched the people on it, the way they walked, the way they stopped to look toward the jail. Twilight, he thought. Won't be long until night. What then?

Jim-Bob asked, "Harvey, how old were you when you were a deputy?"

"A couple or three years older than you are, I reckon."

"Did you ever come up against a situation like this?"

"Never did."

"What would you have done if you had?"

Harvey shrugged. *"Quien sabe?* Who ever knows what he'd do in any situation till he really comes up against it? You study about it, and you think you know yourself. But when the time comes, everything's different. You play it by ear." He paused. "Or maybe you don't play it at-all. You just skin out."

His eyes were on Jim-Bob in a level, honest gaze. "You've been up against it twice today. Once when you jumped up and took Buster Fox, and again when you piled off on top of Tom Singleton. You did fine."

Jim-Bob shook his head. "That wasn't thinkin', either time. I didn't have time to think. I just went ahead. They were bone-headed stunts, both of them. If Buster had held his ground, he could have blown a hole in me you could shove a hat through. And if Tom had had a little pressure on the trigger, he might have killed me without intending to. There was an angel on my shoulder both times, that's all. That's too much luck to keep hopin' for."

Harvey said, "Maybe you're not givin' yourself enough credit. You've got a way of doin' things all of a sudden, and doin' them right."

Jim-Bob moved back into the office and sat

down weakly in a cowhide chair. His shoulders slumped. "Harvey, for the first time in my life, I think I need a drink."

Harvey frowned. Jim-Bob could see sympathy in his eyes. "That won't help you. Either you've got it in you, or you haven't. Whisky won't put somethin' there that wasn't in you to start with." Harvey started to move out the door. "Feel like eatin', Jim-Bob?"

"No."

"You better anyhow. I'll go over and see if Grammon will fry up a steak or somethin' for you." He glanced back into the cell. "I better get somethin' for Fox, too. If things don't work out, there's no use him dyin' on an empty stomach."

Slim Underhill shifted nervously from one foot to the other, and Jim-Bob motioned for him to follow Harvey. For a while Jim-Bob was alone with the prisoner. He moved the straight cowhide chair up close to the front door, where he could keep an eye on the long street. He pulled down the window shades and locked and barred the rear door. Pausing at the rear window, peeking around the shade, he saw a man standing back in the gloom, watching. They've put up their guards early, he thought. He walked back to the chair and sat down. He had taken off the heavy .44 for comfort, but he had a shotgun standing up against the wall within easy reach.

In the short period of peace, then, Jim-Bob had his first chance to relax. Or at least to try. It had been a long and harrowing day, and fatigue washed over him. But his nerves were wound up tight. He could not relax. He knew it would be a long time before he did. He had time now to think, to let his mind dwell on Dan Singleton. Now more than at any time today he felt the full impact of the loss. He tried to blink back the burning tears as he thought of the laughing-eyed boy he had known so long. There was an emptiness, a loneliness in him that he hadn't known since his father had died. He remembered how it had been then, like turning his back on a chapter of his life and starting out alone on a strange new road. He had that feeling again now. He sensed that this was another turning point. From this day forward, nothing would ever be quite the same. This morning he and Dan Singleton had been a pair of big young boys together. Now Dan was gone, and Jim-Bob would never be a boy again. He had finished another chapter.

He saw banker True Farrell striding slowly up the street toward the jail, alone. The old man's gray head was bowed. Trouble rode heavy on his stooped shoulders. He walked up onto the small porch and paused.

"Good evening, Jim-Bob." His voice was weary and thin. This was probably the hardest day of the old man's life.

Jim-Bob stood up in respect. "Come in, Mr. Farrell."

"Thank you." Farrell walked in and stared a moment at Buster Fox in the cell. His veined hands knotted into fists. True Farrell could hate as deeply as anyone else. But he would never be a violent man.

At length he looked back at Jim-Bob. "You didn't find the money." It wasn't really a question. He already knew.

"No, sir. He either hid it or threw it away."

"What's the chance of finding it?"

No use lying to a man like True Farrell. He was level-headed enough to accept fact. "Mighty little, sir. We back-tracked him the best we could, comin' in, and we never saw anything. A couple of the Kendrick hands scouted all over the area where we found him, and so far as I know they never stirred up nothin'. We'll try again, but it'd take the rankest kind of luck. And we been mighty short on luck today."

Farrell nodded. He had probably known before he ever got here. He sank into the sheriff's big chair. When he looked up, his eyes were bleak.

"Jim-Bob, I counted up the loss. We've got to get that money back."

"What if we can't?"

"Then it looks like the bank is finished. And it might take half the town with it. People in a place like Swallowfork don't know how completely their fortunes are tied in with those of the bank. We can't pay our depositors back. We'll have to call in a lot of loans and break people who've been here longer than you or I."

True Farrell seemed to have aged a lot in these

few hours. "I'm not worried so much for myself. I can always find a position in Fort Worth or Dallas or San Antonio. I won't be my own boss anymore, but I won't be hungry. It's the people here that I'm worried about. This is my town. These are my friends. I don't want them hurt, and I don't want to leave."

Jim-Bob said, "Some of your friends are thinkin' about takin' Buster Fox out and hangin' him tonight."

"They mustn't, Jim-Bob. If he dies without showing us where that money is, the town may well die with him."

"Why don't you go tell them that? Why don't you talk to Tom Singleton?"

True Farrell shrugged. "I've already tried. It's as if he were stone deaf. He just sits there, and you can't tell whether he hears you or not. The rest of them are angry too. Whatever Tom does, they'll follow him. He's that kind of man. I've tried, but I can't get them to understand what they're about to do to themselves."

Farrell looked back at Buster Fox. "Think he would tell us if we explained to him how it is?"

"Would you, in his place?"

Farrell sighed. "It was silly of me even to ask. He has a powerful weapon to bargain with, knowing where that money is."

Jim-Bob said, "Only Tom Singleton won't give him a chance to bargain."

It was getting dark in here, and Jim-Bob didn't

125

want to light the lamp. He could still see Buster well enough, though, hunched over in the cell, dirty, bearded, a misery in his pale eyes. With Farrell gone, Jim-Bob got up and walked over to Buster.

"You heard what Mr. Farrell said?"

Buster nodded weakly, not looking up.

Jim-Bob said, "You've got nothin' to gain anymore. Why don't you tell where that money's at? It'd square you that much, and it might make things go a little easier with you."

Buster grunted. "How easy can you go with a hang rope?"

A plea in his voice, Jim-Bob pressed, "Buster, why don't you think of other folks for once? There's a lot of good people in this town goin' to be bad hurt if we don't get that money back."

The outlaw's voice colored with a flare of anger. "What do I care about other people? Nobody ever cared anything about me."

Shaking his head, Jim-Bob turned away from Buster. He knew he could talk until he was hoarse, and he'd never get anything out of that man. He stiffened as he heard a quiet knocking at the back door. Harvey Mills, he thought at first, and he wondered why Harvey would have come back that way instead of through the front. Then he knew it wouldn't be Harvey.

Drawing the .44 out of its holster on the wall, Jim-Bob lifted the bar out of place. He stepped to one side of the door and cautiously opened it an inch. "Who is it?"

"Jim-Bob, it's me." He didn't see the face, for it was dark outside. But he knew the voice. Dencil Fox!

"What do you want, Dencil?"

"I want to see my brother. You know I can't come to the front door."

Jim-Bob held back, not sure he ought to do it. Keeping his back to the wall and the gun up, he opened the door a little wider. "First," he said, "throw your gunbelt in here, and the gun with it."

Dencil's hand showed as he pitched the weapon in. It and the belt slid across the rough board floor.

"Just you now, Dencil," Jim-Bob warned. "Not Pony or Hackberry. And no false moves."

Dencil walked in, his hands up to shoulder height. Jim-Bob quickly shut the door behind him and dropped the bar back in place. He took a quick look at Dencil, decided he was no longer armed, and said, "You can put your hands down now."

"Thanks." Dencil looked quickly toward Buster's cell. Trouble and worry were in his eyes. "How you doin', son?"

Buster's voice was sullen. "How do you think I'm doin'? You come to git me out of here?"

A little of anger tugged at Dencil's mouth. "You got no business bein' in this kind of a jackpot."

"I don't need any lectures. Just git me out."

"I don't know as I can."

"You always did before."

"This is a worse mess than you ever got in before."

Jim-Bob watched Dencil curiously. Even now, knowing him to be a bank robber and a cow thief, it didn't seem to make much difference. He still looked like an ordinary every-day cowboy. He probably had been, once. Jim-Bob could not help but wonder where he had gotten off the road.

He said to Dencil, "You were goin' to rob the bank, the whole bunch of you, isn't that right? Only, Buster tipped over the milk bucket."

Dencil nodded as if it made no difference anyway. He glanced back at his brother. "It was his drinkin' that ruined it. He didn't like the way we had it planned. He got drunk, and we fell out. I don't think he really intended to try and hold it all up my himself. But he got to town, and the more he drank, the easier it looked. So he just bowed his neck and went after it.

"Now, I don't hold with killin'. I've always been able to make a good enough livin' without it. Buster's got a streak in him, though. I don't know where he got it, but it came out in him today." Dencil's forehead furrowed. "Whatever he's done, he's still my brother, Jim-Bob. I don't aim to see him hang."

Jim-Bob could see pain in Dencil's eyes. "It's a lost cause now, Dencil. I'll do what I can. But even if we hold off the lynch mob, the law's certain to hang him. You're not doin' yourself any good stayin' around here. You're a wanted man, just the same as him, and I ought to be lockin' you up. But I like you, and I want you to move on right now, before somebody comes with the supper and I *have* to lock you up."

Dencil's eyes held a queer light as he gazed at Jim-Bob. How much money do you make in a month, son?"

"Forty dollars."

"I got five hundred here in my pocket. As much as you'd make in a year. All you got to do is open that cell door, and it's yours."

Jim-Bob shook his head. "Even if I wanted to, you couldn't get away. Do you think I wouldn't already have taken Buster out if I thought it could be done? They'd run us down. There's men watchin' that back door right now to be sure I don't slip him out."

Dencil's eyes narrowed. "I didn't see any men."

"They were there, and you can bet they saw *you*. Oh, they probably didn't see your face, but they know that one man came in. If more than one man tries to go back out, they'll have a hard time gettin' anyplace. Now go on, Dencil, while you still can. Please."

Regret was in Dencil's eyes. "You're a good kid, Jim-Bob. Any other time . . ." He frowned. "But I reckon you've still got some lessons to learn. One of them is —"

He reached down suddenly and came up with a short-barreled six-shooter out of his boot top.

He swung it into line so abruptly that Jim-Bob hardly had time to move a hand. "One of them is, don't never trust nobody!"

Jim-Bob swallowed, taken completely by surprise.

Dencil said, "Now fetch me them keys, boy. We're lettin' Buster out."

Looking into Dencil's gun, Jim-Bob felt his skin go cold. "I didn't think you'd do that to me, Dencil."

"I didn't want to. I tried money first. Now this is an emergency. Get me them keys."

Buster Fox was standing, gripping the cell bars excitedly. Sweat had broken out on his forehead, and he was grinning in relief.

The key ring still lay on Mont Naylor's desk. Hesistantly Jim-Bob walked over and picked it up. Looking at Dencil, he felt the evening breeze cool the back of his neck as it searched through the open door.

Suddenly, on impulse more than with intention, he pitched the key ring through the door. It landed somewhere out in the sand, in the darkness. He braced himself, half expecting Dencil to shoot him. He turned and saw desperation in Dencil's surprised eyes. For a second or two, Jim-Bob was no farther from death than the thickness of a cigarette paper as Dencil's finger went tight on the trigger.

Dencil's sudden surge of rage passed. "You go out there and get that key!"

Buster's grin had vanished. Dencil's eyes were

unsure. Jim-Bob sensed that he had once again gained the upper hand. He shook his head.

"You can't shoot me, Dencil. One shot would bring them down on this jail like a swarm of hornets. You wouldn't have a chance to get Buster out, or yourself either. Now you better do like I said, get out that back door while you still got time."

Buster saw that Dencil was wavering. He cried out, "Don't go off and leave me, Dencil!"

Dencil allowed the muzzle of the gun to dip a little. The corners of his mouth turned down. Defeat was in his face. "You got a heap of sand, Jim-Bob. It looks like you've won for now. But I'm not leavin' town without Buster. We'll be out there tonight, me and Pony and Hackberry. If that lynch mob gets to crowdin', we'll shoot into it. We'll leave a pile of dead men in that street, boy, like nobody here has ever seen."

His voice was like flint. "And sooner or later, we'll be comin' for Buster. We'll take him peaceful if we can, and otherwise if we have to. You're a good button, Jim-Bob, but I'd kill you to save my brother."

Dencil began backing toward the barred door, stooping down to pick up the gunbelt from the floor. Carefully, his eyes not leaving Jim-Bob, he lifted the bar off. To his brother, he said, "You just hold on, Buster, we'll take care of you." Then, to Jim-Bob, "If you got any friends in that mob, you better stop them before they get to the jailhouse. Otherwise we'll squash them like so many bugs."

He opened the door and vanished into the darkness. Jim-Bob slammed the door and instantly dropped the bar back in place. He turned and leaned heavily against it, his heart hammering away. For a moment he thought his knees would go out from under him. The crushing thought came to him that he was inadequate for the job. This wasn't any make-believe game of sheriffs and outlaws now, no wild daydream of gallantry and adventure. This was a case of real men, angry men, out for vengeance and blood. It was a job that only a man could handle, and Jim-Bob was not sure he was a man yet. Maybe they were right about him. Maybe he *was* just a wet-nosed button packing around a lot more responsibility than he could rightfully handle. Why, of all times, did Mont Naylor have to be out of action on a night like this?

Jim-Bob realized that Buster Fox was watching him, measuring him, and this had a sobering effect. He managed to step away from the wall and stand straight, although the weakness still pulled at his knees. He doubted that Buster could see his face in the gloom, and he was grateful. Bad enough to be so scared that your belly aches. Worse, to know that everyone else knows it.

Chapter Seven

Jim-Bob had no intention of going out into the darkness to hunt for that key ring. There was mightly little chance of finding it in the first place. And he didn't want to take a chance of someone jumping him with no one inside to watch the jail. He knew where Mont kept an extra set of keys in a desk drawer anyway.

Eventually Harvey Mills and Slim Underhill came back bringing supper for Jim-Bob and Buster. They sat down and picked their teeth, waiting. They'd already eaten. Jim-Bob toyed around with his plate a little, not wanting it. He noticed that Buster wasn't eating much, either.

Jim-Bob glanced up at Harvey. "How does it look down the street?"

Harvey frowned, glancing at Slim before he spoke. Slim was shaking his head. "Poor, Jim-Bob, mighty poor. We took a peep in the Tobosa Bar. Tom Singleton's sittin' in the back of it. Not drinkin', not eatin', just sittin' there. And they're gatherin' around him."

"Who?"

"Friends. Maybe some people who don't even know him. Funny how a thing like this draws in even the strangers. And there's some of the

Kendrick outfit on account of the cowboy Fox shot."

It seemed to Jim-Bob that the food was unusually dry. It took a lot of coffee to wash it down. "Is Tom talkin' up a hangin'?"

"He's not talkin' at-all. He don't have to; it's in the air. They'll keep gatherin' down there. After a while he'll just get up and start walkin' thisaway. They'll all follow him."

Jim-Bob felt cold, even though it was a warm night. "I don't reckon you-all will want to be here when that happens."

The partners looked at each other. Finally Harvey said, "You're figgerin' on stayin', aren't you, Jim-Bob?"

"Somebody's got to."

"It'll be a poor place for a man alone. We'll stay with you."

There was little Jim-Bob could say, except "Thanks." He had a hard time keeping his hands still. "Reckon a man could talk to Tom?"

Harvey shrugged. "A man could talk. I don't expect Tom would listen."

"Maybe a man like Walter Chapman . . ."

"The way we heard it, Walter's stayin' out of it. He's sittin' up with Dan's body, over at the parsonage."

"There's bound to be somebody who could talk to Tom."

"Mont Naylor might, but he's not in shape to talk to anyone. We'd just as well face it, Jim-Bob; folks who don't like this thing are stayin' home, keepin' out of the way. Those that are left on the street, they'll come with Tom when he's ready."

Jim-Bob said desolately, "It's hell to just sit here and wait. Somebody's at least got to try. I wish I could talk with Walter."

Harvey said, "Then you go try. We'll watch the jail for you."

"You'll never know how much I appreciate what you-all have done."

Harvey dismissed him with a wave of his hand. "Better get along. There's no tellin' when Tom'll decide to move."

The streets were quiet, deadly quiet. Swallow-fork was not normally a town that went heavy on night life, but even so there was usually more movement on the streets about this time of evening. Now Jim-Bob saw almost none. Not a horse was tied anywhere along the street between the jail and the Tobosa Bar. Everybody knew what was coming. No one wanted to risk his horse breaking away and running off during the excitement, leaving him afoot.

Jim-Bob stood in the shadows beneath the liveoaks, looking around. Presently he saw a movement behind the jail, the flare of a match and the glow of a cigarette. They still had a man watching.

Jim-Bob saw no more movement. Somewhere out there, he knew, Dencil Fox was watching too. Watching and waiting to cut loose with a deadly fire that would leave good men dying in the sandy street. Now, in a way, Jim-Bob regretted that he hadn't locked up Dencil when he had the chance. Yet he hadn't been able to bring himself to do it, to put Dencil in the same hopeless predicament as Buster. He knew he still couldn't, even if he somehow had the chance again.

Jim-Bob walked to the town's white frame church and turned in at the small parsonage that stood beside it. Something moved on the porch. Jim-Bob hauled up short. Then he heard a dog whimper. It was old Ranger. How the dog knew Dan was inside, Jim-Bob would always wonder. The instinct of animals had always been a mystery to him. Whining, the red dog rubbed up against Jim-Bob's leg. Jim-Bob knelt and patted him gently on the head. A great lump swelled in his throat. "It's just you and me now, old partner," he whispered.

He knocked on the door and took off his hat while he waited. The gray-haired minister came in a moment. Momentary surprise was in his eyes. "Come in, Jim-Bob. I thought you'd be tied up at the jail. I know you'll want to see Dan."

Jim-Bob had been trying to keep from thinking of Dan. "I came mostly to see Walter Chapman. Is he here?"

"In the parlor. Come along."

The parlor was lighted by candles, with a white cross standing between them. A plain pine casket rested near the candles. Walter Chapman had been seated in a rocking chair, his head bowed. At sight of Jim-Bob he stood up, sadness in his eyes.

"I didn't expect you, Jim-Bob. But it's good that you got to come."

Jim-Bob moved hesitantly toward the open box and looked inside. He felt a deep chill. This was Dan Singleton, yet it wasn't him at all. The features were his. But this still, cold body in the flickering candlelight was like some clay figure, strangely unreal. The Dan Singleton Jim-Bob had known was gone. He turned away, not wanting to look again. He wanted always to remember the other Dan Singleton. "I came mostly to see you, Walter. You know what's fixin' to happen."

Walter's voice was subdued, almost a whisper. "I know."

"Walter, somebody's got to talk to Tom. You're the only one I know that might make him listen."

Chapman was quiet a little while. Then he said, "What would you want me to tell him, that I think he's doing the wrong thing, that I want him to go home and forget it?"

"Something like that."

Walter's tired face was grim. "How could I tell him he's wrong when I'm not really sure he is?"

Stunned, Jim-Bob said, "Do you mean you think he's right?"

"Who am I to say whether he's right or wrong? I've tried to decide, but I can't. All I know is that we thought the world of this boy, and now he's dead."

A sense of hopelessness gripped Jim-Bob. He hadn't expected a turn-down from Walter Chapman, not even after what Harvey had said. "Walter, no matter what you say, deep inside you know it's wrong."

Walter lowered his head and looked down at the floor. "I guess I do. What's worse, I think I really want it to happen. That makes me a coward of sorts, doesn't it? I sit here tellin' myself I'll have no part in it, that I'm keepin' my hands clean. That makes me worse even than the men who will really go out and do the job. At least they're open and honest with it. I'm a coward and a hypocrite."

Jim-Bob backed toward the door, disappointment heavy on his shoulders. "I'm sorry, Walter."

"So am I, Jim-Bob. But that's the way it is. If anybody talks to Tom, I guess it'll have to be you."

Out on the dark street again, Jim-Bob stood a few moments, trying to make up his mind. He felt a strong temptation to get a horse and ride out and not come back for days. But that wasn't the way John McClain would have done it, or Mont Naylor.

Maybe Walter had a point. Maybe Jim-Bob *could* talk to Tom. He knew the chances were against him. But anything was worth a try. He moved off down the street, the red dog following at his heels.

He expected a cauldron of angry activity at the Tobosa Bar, but he didn't find it. The crowd was there, all right. But it was a grimly quiet group that stood around the bar, some drinking a little, some not drinking at all. The little conversation carried in muffled tones hardly above a whisper. As Harvey had said, Tom Singleton sat at a table alone in the back of the room. No one was talking with him, but Jim-Bob sensed the bond of anger that drew the men to Tom.

All attention riveted on Jim-Bob as he walked through the door. Forty or fifty pairs of eyes quietly took his measure. Jim-Bob felt that weakness come back to him. He tried to muster new strength, to keep the anxiety from showing. He looked over the faces. A few were strangers, but most were people he knew. Cowboys, ranchmen, townspeople. Good men, for the most part, men he had known for years. As individuals, they wouldn't consider killing a man. But now, herding together, they were being caught up in a strong tide of anger and revulsion that was steadily swelling, that would soon break over and crush anything that stood up against it.

His eyes on Tom Singleton, Jim-Bob walked between the other men. They made way for him as he moved, then turned to watch what he would do. He felt no hostility in them. Yet he knew that when the time came they would swarm over him and trample him underfoot if he stepped out in their way. He stopped in front of Tom's table. Tom's dark eyes lifted briefly to him, eyes dulled by grief. Jim-Bob saw recognition there. Then Tom looked down again, his gaze fastening on the table, his mind drawing back to some other time, some other place.

"Tom, I've come to see you." Jim-Bob was surprised at the strength he managed to find in his voice.

Tom made no sign that he had heard.

"Tom, I know what you're figurin' on. You mustn't do it."

Tom said nothing.

"Tom, you know Dan Singleton was the best friend I ever had. We grew up together, rode the same horses, slept in the same bedroll sometimes. He was almost as much a brother to me as he was to you. But I know what you're fixin' to do is wrong."

Tom still didn't look at him, didn't say a word.

"Dan wouldn't approve of it, Tom. He wasn't the kind that would."

Tom looked up at him then, his eyes cold. "How can anybody know now what Dan would approve? He's dead. And your prisoner killed him."

"You know I'm duty-bound to protect Buster Fox. You come up against me tonight and somebody's liable to die."

He didn't dare tell them about Dencil Fox. This bunch would go out into the darkness after him, and somebody would be killed sure enough.

Tom's eyes narrowed. "Do you think you

could kill me, Jim-Bob?"

Jim-Bob stammered for an answer. He had none.

Tom said evenly, "If you stop me, that's what you'll have to do!" He looked down at the table again, withdrawing into the cold shell from which he had so briefly stirred.

Dismayed, Jim-Bob knew he could not budge Tom Singleton. On the contrary, if he stayed here, he probably would stir things up so Tom and these men might come marching even sooner than they otherwise would.

For a moment he considered arresting Tom on the spot and breaking this up that way. But he knew it would be a futile attempt. He would never get Tom out the front door.

"All right, Tom," Jim-Bob said regretfully. "All I can do is warn you." He turned and started out.

"Jim-Bob!" came Tom's stern voice. Jim-Bob stopped and looked back over his shoulder. "What is it?"

Tom said, "I don't want to hurt you, button. Don't you get in my way."

Jim-Bob walked out.

Standing in front of the bar, Ranger beside him, Jim-Bob listened to the voices that had been lifted with his departure. He wondered now if he had done the wrong thing in coming here. The men were louder than they had been before. Maybe his attempt had only stirred them up and hastened the inevitable.

He noticed the many horses tied around the bar, and below it. He might scatter them and create some confusion, but what would it accomplish? It wouldn't last long. Despairing, he turned back toward the courthouse. There was, then, no way he could stop these men from coming. And there would be no stopping them at the jail. If only Mont were able to help . . .

He found himself moving involuntarily toward Dr. Spain's house, where Mont lay. He told himself he should leave Mont alone. Yet Mont was his last flicker of hope. Maybe Mont could suggest something. Only God knew what.

The doctor was skeptical about letting Jim-Bob see the sheriff at all. But he relented. "Just take it easy with him, Jim-Bob. He's not in any shape for excitement. He needs a lot of quiet and rest."

Quiet and rest. The irony of that brought a twist to Jim-Bob's mouth. There wasn't going to be much quiet and rest anywhere in town tonight. Not even for a man in a sickbed. Mont lay on a big bed with heavy iron bedsteads. His square face was drained almost as pale as the pillow upon which his gray head rested. His eyes were closed when Jim-Bob eased into the room, but he opened them a little, awakening slowly.

The doctor murmured in Jim-Bob's ear. "He doesn't know what's shaping up in town tonight. Don't you tell him. He'd lie there and worry about it, and there's nothing he could do."

"He'll hear it anyway, when the noise starts."

"I'm going to give him something to make him sleep."

That jerked another prop out from under Jim-Bob. He had been counting on advice from Mont. Now he couldn't even ask for it.

Mont's voice was barely audible. "Jim-Bob. Glad you came, son."

"I'm tickled to see you lookin' so good, Mont." A lie if he had ever told one. He twisted his hat completely out of shape.

Mont's eyes closed a moment. It must have been an ordeal for him to speak. "How's everything? Prisoner all right?"

"Everything's fine, Mont." Jim-Bob reached up and touched the sheriff's cold hand. "Don't you worry about a thing." He swallowed hard, trying to get a lump down, trying to keep the growing fear out of his voice.

Mont rasped, "You take care of it for me, son. I'll be up and around in a couple of days. Anything comes up, you can handle it."

Jim-Bob nodded, his voice low. "Sure, Mont, I'll handle it. Don't you fret over nothin'." He gripped the sheriff's hand. Then, with a helpless look at the doctor, he turned to the door.

In his small parlor, Dr. Spain reached into a cabinet and took out a bottle and a pair of small glasses. He poured the glasses full and handed one to Jim-Bob. "Brandy. You look like you need it."

"Thanks, doc."

He appreciated the sympathy he saw in the doctor's eyes. Spain was a good man. He had come here many years ago, a gasping consumptive with only weeks to live. This open country with its high climate, its dry air, had turned those weeks into months and the months into years. He could have made a lot more money now in the city somewhere. But it was the city that had so nearly killed him. He preferred to remain in this country where he had found his life. He had all the money he needed to live out here. And he had much more — much that had nothing to do with money.

"Don't worry about Mont, Jim-Bob," Dr. Spain said. "It'll take a lot more than his 'couple of days,' but I promise you he'll make it."

Jim-Bob's lips were tight. "I'm glad. The question now, is, will *I* make it?"

"What can you do?"

"I wish I knew. I was hopin' Mont might tell me."

"And now it's all up to you. A big responsibility for a man so young."

"Too big. I'd just like to saddle me a horse and get out of here as fast as I could run. That would be the easy way."

"You won't do it. You know it wouldn't be the easy way at all. You'd find it the hardest thing you ever did. You'd hate the memory of it. You could run away from Swallowfork and the people here, but you'd never forget. It would be a blot on your conscience as long as you lived."

Jim-Bob's gaze dwelt absently on the glass. "I know. I've got to stay. If I just knew what Mont would do. . . ."

"Jim-Bob, I'm afraid it's too big even for Mont Naylor. He'd try, of course, but in the end he wouldn't be able to stop it. He won't blame you if *you're* not able to. He'll only blame you if he knows you didn't do your best."

Jim-Bob finished the brandy. It warmed him, and he felt a little better. But his hands were still shaky, his stomach uneasy.

Dr. Spain said, "I know it's a tough thing to happen to you, losing your first real prisoner. I remember the very first patient I ever had. He was a drunk who leaned over a saloon balcony to call for another beer. The balcony gave way. I did the best I knew how, and I thought I had him patched up fine. But he died on me."

He smiled then, trying to get through Jim-Bob's somber mood. "Maybe you could set fire to the livery barn or something. Keep them so busy fighting the blaze that they wouldn't have time to worry about your prisoner."

Something hit Jim-Bob. He looked up suddenly and felt the same dart of elation that a falling man feels when his hand grasps something solid, even if only for a second or two. "Doc, maybe you've got it. I might be able to do it."

"Burn the livery barn?"

"No, no, of course not. But something else, something to get them away from the prisoner for a little while."

The idea quickly grew and became a plan. It was a slim ray of hope, and yet it was at least that much. A few moments ago there had been none at all. Jim-Bob pumped the doctor's hand, a nervous smile breaking over his face. "Thanks, Doc, thanks. If it works, I'll get you a whole case of that brandy come Christmas."

He stepped down off the doctor's front porch and hurried toward the livery barn, old Ranger tagging along at his heels.

Old Leather Dryden took care of Mont Naylor's livery barn and wagon yard when Mont was too busy with his peace officer job to do so himself. Like many another old-timer who had cowboyed too long before he quit, Leather had one stiff leg, and his left arm didn't look just right. But he knew his horses.

According to Mont, Leather had seen the elephant and heard the owl hoot in his day. Jim-Bob could only take Mont's word for that. Leather didn't look like it now. He was dried up and played out. He had read some books, and it showed in his talk. Moreover, he had taken to religion, after a fashion. He didn't make an issue of it, but the cowboys who slept in the wagon yard on their visits to town watched their language when Leather was around, and they kept their bottles out of sight.

Right now there wasn't a cowboy anywhere around the barn at all. Leather had it to himself.

From the looks of the horses in the corral, though, Leather had been doing a thriving business earlier. The riders were all over at the Tobosa Bar, Jim-Bob figured.

"Quiet around here," he commented.

Leather nodded gravely. "For a little while maybe. Thought you'd be at the jail." There was question in his eyes.

"Took time out to try to talk to Tom Singleton."

"Didn't do any good, did it?" Leather answered his own question with a shake of his head. "Tom's a single-minded man. And when he gets that mind made up, the gates of hell shall not prevail against him."

Jim-Bob eyed the old cowboy speculatively. "You know what's comin' up tonight, Leather. How do you feel about it?"

Leather frowned, the wrinkles around his eyes deepening and stretching far down his cheeks. "Well, if ever a man deserved hangin', I'd say that man does. But I'm not real sure, Jim-Bob, that any of us, even a judge and jury, has the right to take another man's life away. 'Vengeance is Mine, sayeth the Lord.' One thing for sure, it's wrong to take a man out and string him up the way they're fixin' to do tonight." Conviction burned in his gray eyes. "It's a thing they'll all regret later on. I've tried to tell some of them so. I saw a lynchin' one time. I've spent years tryin' to forget it, but I never have. And I never will."

147

Jim-Bob nodded in satisfaction. "I thought you'd feel that way, Leather, but I had to be sure. There's just a chance we can beat that bunch tonight. Would you be willin' to help?"

"You bet, son. What you want me to do?"

"Dr. Spain gave me the idea. I'm goin' to try to decoy that bunch away so I can slip the prisoner out."

"I'll do anything but set fire to the barn."

Jim-Bob smiled. "That's what Doc suggested, but it's a little drastic. No, I'll need some saddled horses."

Hurriedly he helped Leather catch up and saddle four of Mont's better horses. One pair he picked for sudden speed. The other two were a pair that weren't so fast, perhaps, but could carry a rider for hours at a steady pace and not give out.

"These two," he said, "we'll hide out back yonder, in the dark. If anybody finds them, we're blowed up."

"Nobody'll find them," Leather promised.

"The other two, we'll need up close to the back door of the jail. Give me about ten minutes, Leather, then bring them on. Stay in the dark — don't let anybody see you with them. Ease up under that liveoak *motte* by the courtyard fence. Just wait there and watch the back window. When the time comes, I'll stand by the window and strike a match, like I was goin' to light me a cigarette. Then you bring them horses and come a-runnin'. They'll be taken off of your hands in a hurry."

Leather was shaking his head. "You won't get far, Jim-Bob. That bunch'll run you down."

Jim-Bob said, "That's what the two fast horses are for. Sure they'll run them down, only it'll take a while. And when they do, they'll find it's not me and the prisoner atall. It'll be Harvey Mills and Slim Underhill, if I can get them to swallow the idea. By the time that bunch finds out what happened, I'll be off to a nice head start with Buster Fox. In the other direction."

Admiration showed in Leather's squinched-eyes. "You've got about as much chance as a snowball in h— the hot place. But you know somethin', Jim-Bob? You're lookin' more like your old daddy every day!"

Chapter Eight

Jim-Bob headed back toward the jail, the lonely old Ranger dog not letting him get far ahead. He paused a time or two to spot any lookouts that might be posted. He saw one idling at the closed blacksmith shop, watching the front of the jail. He knew there would be another, or maybe a couple, somewhere out back. Jim-Bob knocked softly on the jail's front door.

"Who is it?" came Harvey's voice.

"Me, Jim-Bob."

The door opened. Jim-Bob slipped in. Slim hurriedly shut the door again, dropping a wooden bar down into place. But not before the dog had gotten in too. Jim-Bob frowned at the bar. "Trouble?"

"Nothin' yet," said Harvey. "But there's been a little prowlin' done outside. Me and Slim thought a mite of precaution would be better than a right smart of cure."

Jim-Bob motioned toward Buster Fox's cell. He could barely see it in the dark. "How's he takin' it?"

"I haven't heard him laughin' much."

Jim-Bob walked back to Buster's cell. He could not see Buster's eyes, but he could almost smell the fear that gripped the man. "Buster, I've got an idea that might save you. But before we try it, I want you to tell me what you did with that bank money."

"You go to hell."

"Buster, you're in a mighty tough spot."

"I'd be in a tougher one if I told you where that money is. It's all I've got to bargain with. You say there's a chance. All right, let's try it. You get me out of here and maybe I'll tell you."

"And maybe you won't."

Buster shrugged. "We'll just have to wait and see."

Harvey Mills showed a lively interest. "What's this chance you're talkin' about? Tom Singleton loosenin' up?"

Jim-Bob shook his head. "Not a bit. I was just hopin' we might outfox him." He dropped his chin and looked up at Harvey and Slim. "You said while ago you'd do anything me or Mont wanted. Does that still go?"

Harvey glanced uncertainly at Slim. "Let's hear the proposition. Mont give you a plan?"

"Mont's in bad shape. He doesn't know what's goin' on. No, this is my idea." He told them about the horses. "When I light the match, Leather will bring them up. I figure if you two bust out of the back door on the run, grab the horses and spur south as hard as you can go, they'll all figure it's me makin' a break toward Dry Creek with the prisoner. They'll take out after you like hounds after a rabbit. When it's clear, I'll slip out with Buster, get the other horses and head north toward Grafton."

Harvey chewed his lip. "There's a flaw in this thing as big as a Chihuahua hat. Them boys are liable to shoot at us, and there's one or two of them that ain't in the habit of missin'."

"I don't think they'll shoot, Harvey. They won't know which one is Buster, and they won't be anxious to kill *me*. The way I figure it, they'll just keep after you till they finally ride you down. But there's a chance I'm wrong. I'd want you to realize that risk before you said yes."

Harvey studied it a little, then looked at Slim "Slim, you been shot at the last day or two?"

Slim shook his head. He seldom spoke, but he was smiling. "Not that I know of."

Harvey shrugged. "All right, Jim-Bob, we'll give it a try. If they *do* shoot us, the joke's on you." His grin died then. "What worries me is you off out in the open country with *him*," he said, pointing his chin at Buster Fox. "I'd sooner carry a rattlesnake in my hip pocket then have him ridden' along beside me."

Jim-Bob said, "I'll watch out for Buster. You two just watch out for Tom Singleton and his bunch."

He pulled out his watch and held it up close to his face, trying to read it in the darkness. "Moon isn't up yet, but it soon will be. We need to be on our way before it comes." He frowned at the two men. "You sure about this now? I wouldn't want you to think I was tryin' to pressure you into it."

Harvey said testily, "We told you, didn't we?"

Jim-Bob held out his hand. "All right then. Lead them as far as you can, but if it gets too tight, don't take any unnecessary risk. Good luck to you."

Each man shook Jim-Bob's hand. "Send us a letter from Grafton," grinned Slim.

Jim-Bob raised the shade on the rear window and struck a match. He heard the quick strike of hoofs. "He's comin'," he said. Harvey slid the bar off and pushed open the door.

"Run for it," Jim-Bob whispered urgently.

Harvey and Slim jumped out over the back steps and hit the ground running. Watching from inside, Jim-Bob spotted a quick movement in the shadows. A man trotted out into the open, waving his hand in excitement. "Stop there!" he shouted futilely. "You ain't gonna do this!"

The two men kept running. The lookout shouted louder, "They're gettin' away! Help me, you-all! Stop them, somebody!"

The man drew his gun and leveled it. Jim-Bob sucked in a sharp breath. Then, as he had hoped, the lookout evidently changed his mind, afraid he might hit the wrong man. He fired into the air. "You-all come help me! They're gettin' away!"

Leather came in a hurry, leading the two horses. Harvey and Slim grabbed the reins and swung up, keeping themselves bent low. They spurred out before they even had their right feet well into the stirrups. Leather faded back into the shadows. Jim-Bob knew he would return to the livery barn.

The lookout kept shouting and firing into the air, running afoot after the two riders. Though he could not catch them himself anymore, he had created an explosion of excitement down the street. Jim-Bob could tell from the noise that men were boiling out of the Tobosa Bar. He could hear drumming of hoofs as cowboys caught up their horses. Several men ran by the jail afoot, heading south toward the excitement.

Jim-Bob unlocked the cell door. It squealed as he swung it open, and the sound raised the hair at the back of his neck. "Come on, Buster. We better get out of here while all the excitement is down the street. Some of those left behind are liable to pop in here directly, lookin' for somebody they can raise hell with."

Buster Fox quavered. "What if they catch us out there?"

"Safer out there in the dark than it'll be in here. Grab your hat and let's skin out."

As Buster reached the cell door, Jim-Bob was ready with a set of handcuffs. He locked Buster's wrist to his own, only a short chain between them. He motioned with his .44. "Don't you take any foolish notions when we get out there. Any kind of commotion and they'll be on us."

Buster almost stumbled on old Ranger. The dog stuck close beside Jim-Bob. Jim-Bob whispered, "Go home, Ranger. Go home." But the dog paid him no heed. Gripping the gun tightly in his free right hand, Jim-Bob led Buster out the door into the darkness. He hugged up against the building and worked his way along in the deep shadows as far as he could.

"Those trees yonder," he whispered. "Duck down and let's get to them."

He waited just a moment, taking a long look and seeing no sign of anyone close by. Then he sprinted across the open space, Buster right beside him. They reached the deep shadows again and crouched to catch their breath and listen. Jim-Bob and Buster were almost afraid to breathe. But Ranger squatted unconcernedly beside them, panting for the whole town to hear.

Buster whispered urgently, "Get rid of that dog!"

"I can't." Jim-Bob wished Ranger would leave; but he knew no way to send him off without raising a racket about it.

From down the street, around the livery barn and the Tobosa Bar, he could still hear frenzied activity. Men were catching their horses and riding out in the chase. From farther south, well out of town, came the fading sound of running horses and shouting men. Occasionally one of these men would fire into the air as a signal to guide those later ones still trying to catch up. The shots were trailing farther away.

"Stop breathin' so hard, Buster," Jim-Bob spoke quietly. "I'm just as scared as you are."

He thought he saw a movement at the jail. He made out the form of a man entering the open back door. He couldn't be sure, but he thought another man was waiting outside.

"We got out of there just in time," he whispered.

The man came back out of the jail and headed south like the rest, afoot and in a hurry. Jim-Bob could tell that another man or two were with him.

He tugged at the handcuff. "Come on, we better ease toward the livery barn and get our own horses."

Buster asked anxiously, "How long do you reckon your friends can keep them led off?"

"No tellin'. Just accordin' to how the luck runs. We better be doin' some runnin' ourselves."

Buster said worriedly, "I wonder where Dencil's at? He promised he'd be around."

"I figure he's followin' that lynch mob, him and Pony and Hackberry. They'll have it in mind to rescue you when the mob catches up to you and me. They'll get as big a surprise as the rest when it turns out it's Harvey and Slim after all."

He couldn't see Buster's face, but he could sense the prisoner's disappointment. "Looks like it worked out pretty good all around," Jim-Bob commented. "Got rid of the mob and Dencil too. Now let's mosey."

They took the long way to the corrals, staying in the shadows most of the time, keeping well away from lamplight that spilled out of many windows along the street. By the time they reached the back side of the wagon yard, the excitement there was over. The last rider had caught his horse and had ridden away, or else had given up and gone back to the bar. A sharp smell of dust lay heavy in the air. Angry talk floated down from around the Tobosa. Frustrated, the cowboys were probably making plans not only for what they'd do to Buster when they caught him, but also for that smart-aleck kid deputy.

"I don't reckon I'm any more popular up there right now than you are, Buster," he said. "Let's go easy now. We tied the horses in this little mesquite thicket out back of the corrals."

He moved as quietly as he could, but it seemed to him that the pair of them were as noisy as a bunch of big steers, feet brushing through the heat-dried grass, boots crushing an occasional twig or dead limb that had fallen from a mesquite.

They had just reached the thicket when Jim-Bob saw a man moving toward him. His heart leaped, and he brought up the gun. Ranger began barking at the man. Jim-Bob thought his legs would give way.

"Jim-Bob," the man whispered. Jim-Bob recognized old Leather Dryden. He lowered the gun, his heart still pounding away. The breath was nearly gone from him

"Hush up, Ranger," Jim-Bob hissed. "Git," Then to Leather he said, "My Lord, Leather, I like to've shot you."

157

"I had to be sure somebody didn't find the horses. Nobody saw you?"

"We wouldn't be here if they had."

Buster was cursing softly. "That lousy dog. He'll be the death of us yet. If I had a gun I'd kill him."

Jim-Bob replied, "I wouldn't swap him for a dozen of you. Ranger, go on home!"

The dog reluctantly moved out a ways and stopped to watch.

Leather said, "I put Mont's saddlegun and scabbard on your saddle. You may need it."

"Thanks, Leather. I didn't think of it."

Jim-Bob untied the horse he had selected for Buster. He unlocked the cuff from his own wrist and snapped it around Buster's other wrist.

"Mount up."

Buster did, and Jim-Bob swung into his saddle. He loosened the hornstring and shook out a loop in his rope. This he dropped over Buster's shoulders and drew it up around the man's belly.

"Just to supplement the handcuffs," he said. "You try anything and you'll get yanked out of that saddle."

He leaned down and shook Leather's tough old hand. "Thanks, Leather. Just one more favor — when Doc Spain approves, would you go tell Mont what we've done? I expect it'll make him rest easier."

"Mont'll be proud of you, son. But you're a long way from Grafton, and you better git ridin'. God go with you."

Jim-Bob pulled his horse around and headed him straight west at the beginning. Out this way was only a scattering of houses and the least chance of being seen. Buster did not lag, for he knew Jim-Bob meant business with that rope. Jim-Bob looked behind him. As he thought, Ranger trotted along at a discreet distance. He stopped to order the dog home again, but he knew it was useless. Ranger had lost Dan. He didn't want to lose Jim-Bob.

The two riders kept their horses in an easy walk as they skirted the houses. Jim-Bob thought they were going to make it without incident. But then the dogs picked them up. Several dogs moved in and began to bark at the horses. Buster said fearfully, "They hear them dogs."

Jim-Bob held his breath. He saw a man open a door and peer out into the darkness. He hauled up short and held still, hoping the man would not see him and Buster. The man stood on his front steps and looked in their direction, where the dogs were setting up a racket.

"What's goin' on out there?" the man called. "Who is it?"

He started to move their way. Jim-Bob didn't think he had actually seen them yet. Just then old Ranger declared himself into the game. He tore into one of the dogs with a vengeance. For a moment it was a madhouse of yelping and excited barking.

The man evidently satisfied himself that it was

nothing but a strange dog trespassing in the neighborhood. He growled something about thinning out a bunch of dogs one of these days and went back into his house.

Jim-Bob exhaled slowly and wiped cold sweat from his face. "I knew Ranger would amount to something someday if we left him alone."

He tugged on the rope, and the two started riding again. Behind them, Ranger was still entertaining the other dogs, holding them at bay. "We'll probably lose him now. By the time he gets through back there, we'll be gone. He'll turn around and go home."

Jim-Bob tried to listen for sounds of the mob after Slim and Harvey, but the continued barking drowned out any distant shots that might otherwise have carried this far. By now, he figured, the mob was just riding hard, trying to catch up to those two fast horses. They wouldn't be doing much shooting.

Finally Jim-Bob and Buster passed the last shack on the east edge of town. "From here on out, Buster, it's open country. We better start tryin' to make some time."

He reined north then, straight north toward Grafton. He had it in mind to intersect the wagon road somewhere up ahead and follow it. He moved into an easy lope. Buster was a little slow in following. The rope drew up taut. Buster spurred and moved abreast of Jim-Bob.

"How about this rope?" he complained. "Have we got to leave it on?"

"If you were me, would you take it off?"

Buster did not reply to that, and the rope stayed around him. They stayed in an easy lope for a while. Jim-Bob wanted to put as much distance behind them as he could, yet he knew he could not afford to overtax the horses. If he did that, he had just as well give up before he started. There might come a time, later tonight, when a little reserve strength, a little extra speed, would be a matter of life or death.

They rode up on top of a gentle rise. Jim-Bob drew up a moment, taking a last look at the lamp-lighted town which lay at some distance behind them. He stepped out of the saddle so that he might hear better any noise from behind them. He heard nothing. Damnation, he thought, he would give a month's pay just to know what was going on back there.

Not far ahead would be the wagon road to Grafton. Coming in at a tangent as they were they would strike it somewhere on the flat that lay below them. Jim-Bob would be glad to get on the road. No matter how well a man thought he knew the country, he was likely to stray some and put in a few extra miles trying to ride across it in the dark. Especially a place as far away as Grafton. The moon was coming up. It was getting light enough now that Jim-Bob could make out individual mesquite trees, coal-black against a silver ground. He and Buster hadn't gotten out of town any too soon. "Let's get to the road, Buster. We've killed all the time we can afford."

They were within a couple of hundred yards of the road when Jim-Bob heard the horses coming. He jerked on the reins and nodded toward a pair of mesquites nearby. He and Buster pulled up behind them and waited. Not letting his eyes roam far from Buster, he got down to watch. He made out three men, swinging along in an easy lope. Jim-Bob's horse started to nicker. Jim-Bob reached up quickly and grabbed the animal's nose, stopping the sound. He held his own breath until the riders were past them and out of sight in the dim moonlight.

"Cowboys on their way home," he said. "Probably missed the show in town. They don't know how close they just missed one here." He got back into the saddle. "Guess we can't use the road after all," he said regretfully. "We'll have to take out across country."

A little flicker of hope came to Buster Fox. "There was three of them. You know, that just might be old Dencil, and Pony and Hackberry."

The thought gave Jim-Bob a sudden jolt. He hadn't considered that. "It can't be, Buster. They're bound to be out chasing after that mob. We fooled them like we fooled everybody else."

"Dencil's a hard man to fool. He might just be a little too smart for you, boy."

"Why don't you holler and find out?" Jim-Bob challenged Buster.

That put an end to it, as far as Buster was concerned. But it gave Jim-Bob something new to worry about. What if he *hadn't* fooled Dencil?

Chapter Nine

They angled westward awhile. Jim-Bob wanted to put some distance between them and the wagon road. It wasn't bad for a while, because the land was mostly gentle, flat, or rising and falling only a little. Occasionally they moved through patches of brush, and he kept a close watch on Buster Fox.

In time he sensed that Buster had shaken the heavy anxiety that had gripped him. Buster sat straighter in the saddle, surer of himself. He even began to hum.

"I don't know what you've got to feel so happy about," Jim-Bob commented dryly.

"If you'd just got out of a hangin', you'd feel good too."

"You mean I got you out of it."

Buster replied flatly. "You got nothin' to brag about. You was the one got me into it in the first place. Maybe someday I'll find the way to thank you right and proper. And I don't think you'll enjoy it much."

"You're not goin' to get much chance for anything anymore that you can't do in jail, Buster. You've got a fair trial comin' to you, then a good *legal* hangin'. If I was in your boots, I don't know how much hummin' I'd do."

Buster gave him a dry laugh. "You really think they'll hang me? Boy, the snow'll be three feet deep here the Fourth of July before they ever hang Buster Fox."

"I don't see that you've got any way out of it."

"I got two ways out. One of them is me, and the other is my brother Dencil. I been in mighty few spots in my day that I couldn't get out of by myself. And them few, Dencil took care of. Don't you go buyin' any flowers for me, boy. It'll be a long time before ever I need them."

Buster began to sing a bawdy dancehall tune about a girl in a red dress. Jim-Bob took it as long as he could then flamed. "Shut up, Buster. Doesn't it bother you at-all, knowin' that you've killed two men today, two good young men that never hurt you or nobody else?"

Buster shrugged. "They won't come back to life, me worryin' over them. A dead man is dead, boy, and you'd just as well forget about him."

Jim-Bob's teeth ground together. "I'm not for-gettin' them, Buster, especially not the one in the bank. He was the best friend I ever had."

Buster said, "That's tough. But he ought to've known what he was gettin' into when he went to work in a bank. Bank's a dangerous place for a man to be, boy, all that money around. He ought to've worked in a mercantile or somethin', and he wouldn't have gotten his fool self hurt."

Jim-Bob reined up suddenly. The rope snapped taut on Buster's belly. Buster jerked out of the saddle and landed with a hard thud on the ground. It jarred him. For a moment he sat there, numb. Angry himself, Jim-Bob could feel the burn of Buster's glare across the ten feet that separated them.

"What do you think you're doin'?" Buster demanded. "Did you pull me away from that mob just so you could kill me yourself?"

Jim-Bob's voice was brittle. "Don't tempt me, Buster."

Buster swore under his breath. He got up stiffly and rubbed his hip. "Crazy kid, there ought to be a law against anybody like you packin' a star. You could kill somebody."

"Awful easy," Jim-Bob said. "Come on, let's go."

They rode a couple of hours then without speaking. Jim-Bob gradually eased the direction of travel back toward the north star. He kept Buster riding a little in the lead, so that never would Jim-Bob's gaze need to be away from him, never would Buster be able to spur in suddenly and surprise him. He had learned that lesson from Jace Dunnigan. It was a mistake he would never make again.

Riding, Jim-Bob found himself growing curious about Buster, wondering what it was that made him so quick to kill. Finally he said, "Buster, I been tryin' to figure you out. For the life of me, I can't. How does a man get off the track the way you did? What ever made an outlaw of you?"

Strangely, the question seemed to please Buster, seemed to touch the braggart in him. "You really consider me an outlaw, boy?"

"What else?"

"How many real outlaws did you ever see?"

"I was out with the C Bar wagon one time when a man came ridin' up about dark and asked if he could spend the night with us. I was just a button and had a pretty good-sized bedroll, so Tom Singleton put him in with me. Next mornin', when he left, the other boys told me he was Alkali Gotcher from out west of the Pecos. I didn't sleep good for three or four nights afterwards."

Buster laughed. "Alkali Gotcher! Who ever heard of anybody losin' sleep over a counterfeit like that? His blood would turn to clabber if he ever went up against a real badman."

"He looked tough enough to me."

Buster snickered. "Counterfeit."

Jim-Bob's nose wrinkled. "You didn't look so tough yourself yesterday when we took you. Or tonight when it looked like Tom Singleton was fixin' to get you. I'll bet you'd have cried like a baby if they'd taken you out."

He heard Buster's sharp intake of breath. "Shut up, boy. Maybe I'll show you just how tough I can really get."

"What's the matter, Buster? Do you hate the whole world?"

"This world owes me a lot, boy. I still got a good many debts out, and I aim to collect on them."

166

"And kill innocent people doin' it?"

"Let them watch out for themselves. There ain't nobody ever done anything for Buster Fox."

"Dencil did."

"That's different. He's my brother. Brothers are supposed to look out for each other."

"Dencil told me how you two were on your own as kids. But so was I. Lots of people were good to me. Didn't anybody ever help you, Buster?"

Buster scowled. "Not without damn well lettin' me know they were doin' me a favor and that I owed them somethin'. There never was anybody cared anything for me except Dencil. Not even our old man and old woman."

Jim-Bob didn't prod him, but Buster seemed to want to talk now. "First it was the old man. He was a faro dealer. I remember how he and the old woman used to drag us around from town to town when we was just little bitty buttons. Sometimes they would move us in the middle of the night. They hated each other, and I think they hated us. First it was the old man, just took off one night and never did come back. Then the old lady. We went three days without anything to eat, waitin' for her to show up again. She never did.

"There wasn't anybody wanted us. Folks would feed us a meal and start us on our way to get shed of us, hopin' somebody else would pick us up so we wouldn't be left on their hands. We was both too little to work, people said. So when we got hungry enough, we'd steal. We got awful thin sometimes, but we never did starve. Finally we got big enough to really work. We'd stay on a ranch awhile, then they'd decide they didn't like me. They always liked Dencil well enough; it was *me* they picked on. Me and Dencil, we found out how easy it was when we left a place just to take a few of their cattle with us. We never did have much trouble selling them to somebody.

"Dencil always could tell who was a likely prospect to buy our cattle. He said he could tell by lookin' in their eyes. Honest people, most of them was supposed to be. But Dencil could always tell. They knew the brands had been changed, but they hadn't done it themselves, and that made a difference. If anybody ever asked, why, they bought them cattle, and they had a bill of sale to show for it."

Buster laughed harshly. "Honest people! I'm tellin' you, boy, most people are just as crooked as those of us they call outlaws, only they keep it covered up with a coat of white paint. Just let them have a chance to make some fast money and you'll see how quick that white paint turns black."

Jim-Bob said, "A man generally finds what he's lookin' for. There's enough bitterness in you to sour all the milk cows in Texas."

Buster looked scornfully at Jim-Bob. "Maybe you think *you're* honest. Maybe it made you feel real holy tonight when you turned down

168

Dencil's offer of money to let me out. But you turned it down because it wasn't enough, that's all. If he'd made it big enough, you'd have grabbed it and run. You'd find out you're a counterfeit just like the rest. The only difference in anybody is the price it'll take to make them sell out."

Jim-Bob just shook his head. He still could not muster any sympathy for Buster. But maybe he understood a little better what made Buster so ready to lash out at anyone who came near him. He kept the horses moving at a good clip, trotting them awhile, then loping them some, trying to make all the time that he could. But eventually it began to tell on the horses. Jim-Bob could feel his brown laboring to keep up the pace.

He thought he knew about where he was, but in the night this way, in country he hadn't ridden over a great deal, it would be easy to miss the mark. In one way he wished for daylight, that he could know for certain. Yet again, with daylight he would lose the protective cover of darkness that had gotten them this far.

He had intended all along to stop at George Thorn's TX ranch and get a pair of fresh horses. The way he had been figuring it, they ought to reach there about sunup. Maybe earlier. Trouble was, they might pass it up in the dark. Then they would have to make the whole trip on these same tired horses.

"We've made good time," he told Buster, "but it's takin' too much out of the horses. From here on we better just stay in a trot and save them all we can. We'll bear a little to the east and try to strike the dry fork of Paint Horse Creek. If we find it and follow it, we can get ourselves some fresh mounts.

Buster's voice sharpened in alarm. "Where we goin'?"

"Friend of mine has got a ranch up ahead of us."

Doubtfully Buster said, "Those were friends of yours in town, too."

"You gettin' scared again? I thought you were the tough one."

Resentment was in Buster's reply. "You'll see how tough I am. Sooner or later, I promise I'll show you."

Eventually they came upon the fork. Jim-Bob motioned with his hand, and they headed north up its west bank. Summer had shut the rainfall off and slowed the flow of the springs. Water was not running down the bed of the creek now, but all the potholes still held water from the last rain.

Jim-Bob could tell by the stars that the morning hours were wearing along. Luck was running with them, he thought. All that way and they hadn't stumbled onto anything that might look like trouble. Not even so much as a sheep camp.

Dawn was setting the brush afire off the eastern line of hills when Jim-Bob saw the TX headquarters stretched out ahead of them. "That's it, Buster," he said. "Keep on the look-out for some horses."

In a moment Buster pointed. "There's a bunch right yonder."

They moved toward the horses. This was a set of George's broncs, but Jim-Bob knew they weren't going to do any better. He threw up his hand and yelled, *"Hy-yaah!"* The animals turned and headed for the house in a long trot.

"You a pretty good bronc rider, Buster?"

"Never did care much for it. Broke horses was always easy to get."

"Broncs is all we're likely to find here. George Thorn breaks horses for a livin'. He says he sees no future in keepin' them around after they're gentle. One ever gets to where he won't pitch, George sells him."

Nearing the corrals and George's simple frame house, Jim-Bob said quietly, "Whoa up a little. We better make sure first that George hasn't got company."

He looked until he was satisfied, not missing the tension in Buster's face. "All right," he said, "looks clear."

The loose broncs headed straight through an open gate into a corral. Jim-Bob followed along, watching the house. Lamplight shone through the kitchen window. These ranch people never let daylight catch them asleep.

Jim-Bob pitched Buster a little slack in the rope. "Get off and shut the gate behind those broncs."

When Buster had remounted, they rode the extra distance to the house.

171

"George!" Jim-Bob called, "George Thorn!"

Sue-Ellen was the first to appear in the doorway, wiping her hands on a flour-sack apron. She saw who it was, smiled, then caught herself. "Jim-Bob McClain, what do you mean ridin' up here this time of mornin' and hollerin' like that? For all you know, folks might be asleep."

Jim-Bob came close to grinning at her. "Not around this place, they wouldn't."

Sue-Ellen noticed Buster then, and the rope around his waist. Her eyes widened, and she said nothing more.

George Thorn hobbled out onto his little porch, coffee cup in his hand. He stopped there until he recognized Jim-Bob in the growing light of dawn. "Mornin', Jim-Bob," he said pleasantly. "If you'd come an hour earlier, you'd have caught me in bed." He stared curiously at Buster Fox, at the rope and the handcuffs. "What the Sam Hill you got there?"

"Prisoner, George. Takin' him to Grafton to a safe jail. We need to swap for fresh horses. I'll bring yours back later."

The stiffened old bronc rider frowned at Buster Fox. "I'll bet he's the one that killed Dan Singleton and that boy out at the Kendrick outfit. We heard about it last night."

Jim-Bob nodded. "He's the one. They were fixin' to lynch him."

George's wind-burned face twisted. "Can't say I blame them any."

Jim-Bob said sharply, "He's a prisoner,

George. Don't you get any idea . . ."

George Thorn shook his gray head. "Don't worry, thinkin' is all I'd do about it. Sure, you can have some horses. Sue-Ellen, you fix them some breakfast while we get their saddles changed."

Jim-Bob protested. "No time for that, George. They're liable to be along directly, lookin' for us."

"Coffee's done fixed, and she'll have eggs and bacon ready by the time we swap saddles." Handing Sue-Ellen his empty cup, George stepped down off the porch and glanced toward a small shack back of the house. "Wish Chum Lawton would get up of a mornin' without me callin' him three times. He's a fair-to-meddlin' bronc rider but the laziest one ever I seen."

Jim-Bob and Buster rode back to the corral. George hobbled along hurriedly, reaching the gate about the same time they did. He unlatched it and held it open for them to ride in.

Jim-Bob thought about letting Buster help change the saddles, but he decided against it. With half a chance, Buster might try anything. A swinging girth with its brass buckle could be a powerful weapon. Jim-Bob unlocked one of the cuffs from Buster's wrist and snapped it shut again on a post. "That'll hold you while we saddle up."

Jim-Bob unsaddled his own horse. George turned loose Buster's. He looked at the horses Jim-Bob had brought in and said, "I'll have to apologize a little for them. They won't be as good as what you were ridin'. They've been gentled a little, but they're still mostly bronc."

"Just pick us what you think are the best two," Jim-Bob said.

George swung his loop in a figure eight and caught out a young sorrel. "I'd say this is the top horse. Next one is that dun yonder. He's liable to bow up a little and might even pitch a jump or two, but he's the best-goin' bronc here."

Jim-Bob mused, "Better let Buster have him. I'd hate for him to break in two with me and let Buster get away while I had my hands full."

Buster glared at him, not relishing the idea of getting on a bronc.

George said, "It'd tickle me to see this dun bust him right half in two. Only I don't expect he'll be that bad."

By the time they got saddled and led the horses back to the house, Chum Lawton had gotten dressed and was washing his face and hands in the tin wash basin at the edge of the porch. Drying his face, he eyed Jim-Bob and the prisoner speculatively. "Who caught him for you, Jim-Bob?"

Yesterday Jim-Bob would have flared. Now Chum just left him cold. After what he had been through, Chum was no worse than a gnat buzzing around his ear. Jim-Bob said, "I had help. Better men than you'll ever be."

Sue-Ellen stepped to the door, worriedly watching the two. She saw that there was no anger in Jim-Bob's face, and she eased some. "Breakfast's on the table. You-all better come."

Jim-Bob pulled out a chair for Buster and motioned him to sit down. As he had done at the corral, he unfastened one cuff and relocked it to a table leg. "You can eat with one hand."

Buster colored. "You don't trust nobody, do you?"

"If you had the chance, you'd run like a rabbit."

Buster grunted, "And I expect you'd shoot me like one."

Bluntly Jim-Bob said, "I'd try."

Sue-Ellen had scrambled the eggs. Jim-Bob spooned out a big helping for Buster and added some bacon. "You better eat good. We still got a long ways to go."

Bolting his food, Jim-Bob surreptitiously watched Sue-Ellen. Any time he looked down, he could feel her brown eyes studying him. Funny, he never had especially noticed how downright good-looking she was. He realized he had always needed to compare her with Tina Kendrick, and alongside Tina's cameo beauty, most any girl would look plain.

Only, what good was beauty when there was nothing beneath it?

Sue-Ellen said, "I heard you tell Dad this is the man who did all those things over at Swallowfork yesterday." When Jim-Bob nodded, she asked, "What was it you said about them tryin' to hang him?"

175

Briefly Jim-Bob told what had happened.

Sue-Ellen said, "Dan Singleton was always your best friend, wasn't he?"

Jim-Bob nodded soberly.

There was admiration in her voice. "You risked a lot to save this man, even though he murdered Dan. I used to worry about when you'd ever grow up, Jim-Bob. I don't think I'll worry anymore."

Jim-Bob looked at her, and he felt his face warm a little.

Chum Lawton had been listening, his ears perked up. "They were really after him, were they, Tom Singleton and the rest?"

"They wanted him pretty bad."

Chum almost smiled. "Those boys are goin' to be real mad at you when you get back to town." Easy to tell that Chum enjoyed the thought.

Regretfully Jim-Bob said, "I imagine so."

"I expect they'd be grateful to anybody who was to put a crimp in your scheme."

Suddenly worried, Jim-Bob said, "Don't you figure on tryin' anything, Chum."

Chum grinned. "I was just supposin'. Clever as you are, there couldn't anybody put much over on you, could they?"

Jim-Bob lost taste for the breakfast. Funny, the way Chum Lawton could spoil anything for him. That buzzing gnat had turned into a barking dog.

Sue-Ellen was concerned over something. "Dad, do you think all this might have something to do with those men who came by here this morning and got fresh horses?"

Jim-Bob nearly dropped his coffee cup. "What men?"

George shrugged. "I wouldn't hardly think so. It wasn't no posse or mob or anything. Just three men."

Three men! Jim-Bob's stomach went cold. "What did they look like?"

"Tougher than a leather boot. They left maybe thirty or forty minutes before you rode up. They drove horses into the pen and started changin'. Didn't say howdydo or thank-you-ma'am or nothin'. I got up and walked out there to see what was goin' on. I looked at them, and they looked at me, and I just decided to keep my mouth shut. Besides, they was leavin' better horses than they was takin'."

Jim-Bob's heartbeat quickened. "George, did any one of them look like him?" He nodded toward the prisoner.

George's brow furrowed as he studied Buster. "You might say so. Fact of the matter, I'd say he sure did." His gaze lifted to Jim-Bob. "After you, are they?"

Jim-Bob nodded bleakly. The world had risen up and hit him in the face. But how? How could they? "I'd have bet the best pair of boots in Swallowfork that I threw them off the trail just like I did Tom's bunch."

Buster Fox was grinning. "So old Dencil didn't take the bait after all? I told you you'd get no place messin' around with the Foxes, boy."

"Who's Dencil?" Sue-Ellen asked.

"His brother."

She took in a long breath, fear in her eyes. "Then he's liable to be waitin' for you somewhere up ahead?"

Jim-Bob shook his head. "Not *liable*, Sue-Ellen. He *will* be."

She frowned, thinking something out. Then: "Dad, he can't go on alone. We've got to go along and help him."

Jim-Bob protested, "No, Sue-Ellen, it's *my* job."

George said, "She's right, Jim-Bob. You up against three men, plus this one, you won't have a chance."

Jim-Bob said, "I didn't go into this thing blindfolded. I knew what I might come up against before I ever started. I won't let you go, George. As for Sue-Ellen . . ." He shook his head.

Sue-Ellen said, "I can shoot as straight as any man you can put up against me."

Jim-Bob replied, "And you can get shot, just like any man. Forget about it, I tell you."

It occurred to him that nobody had suggested he take Chum Lawton along. Chum himself hadn't made the offer, either. Jim-Bob wouldn't have accepted, even if he had.

"Hurry up there, Buster," Jim-Bob ordered. "We got to go." He shoved his own plate back. He couldn't help noticing how unsteady his hands were. Buster gulped the last of his coffee. "Any old time, boy. We don't want to keep Dencil waitin'."

Jim-Bob unlocked the cuff from the tableleg and snapped it back on Buster's wrist. He nodded toward the door. Buster stood up and moved out.

"Thanks for the breakfast, Sue-Ellen," Jim-Bob said warmly. He wanted to leave, yet somehow he couldn't, not without saying something more to her. "I'm grateful for your offer, Sue-Ellen. Even if I can't take it, I'll never forget that you made it."

She smiled. "You'll accept it. We'll follow along behind you, and you can't make us go back."

Jim-Bob swore under his breath. Stubborn woman. How could you argue with one like that? They were halfway to the corral when Jim-Bob heard Chum Lawton yell, "Stop right where you're at, Jim-Bob."

He whirled and saw a six-shooter in Chum's hand.

Chapter Ten

"Chum, what do you think you're doin'?"

"I was just thinkin' how popular a man would be if he was to take your prisoner back to Tom Singleton and the men that want him so bad. I was just thinkin' maybe it would make a man popular enough to win an election for sheriff, if he was of a mind to run."

"Elect a man because he turned a prisoner over to a lynch mob? Chum, you're out of your head."

"No, Jim-Bob, just *usin'* my head. You raise them hands up. Raise them real high."

Grudgingly Jim-Bob complied. "I'll get you for this, Chum. I'll see you in the pen for it if it's the last thing ever I do."

Chum grinned. "No you won't. My friends won't let you. You won't do a thing to me. I'll be the sheriff of this county first thing you know, and *you'll* be the one bustin' broncs."

Jim-Bob glanced at Buster. The cockiness had vanished from the outlaw again. He was in a tough spot here, and he knew it.

Chum said, "Fox, you go on toward that corral, and don't you make any false moves. I reckon they'd almost as soon have you dead as alive."

Jim-Bob said grittily. "And you wouldn't mind bein' known as the one who shot him."

Chum replied, "Not a bit, Jim-Bob. Not a bit."

Jim-Bob thought he knew what would happen if Chum got away with this. He would shoot Buster before he had gone half a mile with him. It was the old Mexican border custom, *ley fuga*. Shot trying to escape. Nobody would ever contest him about it. Nobody but Jim-Bob.

Jim-Bob abruptly made up his mind. He would see just how far Chum was willing to go. He suddenly stepped in front of Buster Fox. "You can't shoot him now, Chum, not without shootin' me first."

Chum said, "Step aside, Jim-Bob, I don't aim to hurt you."

"You don't *dare* to hurt me." He eased toward Chum his hand outstretched. "Better give me that gun, Chum."

Chum's grin fell away. His face tightened. He lifted the gun a little. "I'm tellin' you, Jim-Bob, don't you come any closer. All I want is Fox. I don't want to have to shoot *you*."

"You can't have him. And you know what'll happen if you shoot me. Like it or not, I'm an officer of the law. They'll take you out and hang you, Chum. Hang you up there and choke the life out of you. Ever see a man hang, Chum? You wouldn't like it." Truth was, Jim-Bob never had seen a hanging himself, and he didn't ever care to. But anything was fair now if it would keep

Chum flustered until Jim-Bob could get within reach of him. "Go on, Chum," Jim-Bob challenged, "pull that trigger and get me out of the way." He tried to keep his face straight, but inside he was wound up tight as a fiddlestring. Chum might just be crazy enough to do it.

But Chum backed up a step, and then another. Jim-Bob saw that he had Chum on the run. Suddenly he took two long strides and caught up to the man. He grabbed the gun.

Chum held on, struggling with him. Chum cursed as they fought, his face reddening in rage and frustration. Both men gripped the gun, each trying to throw the other off balance. Sweat broke out on Jim-Bob's forehead as he strained. Then he got a solid footing and threw his shoulder into Chum's stomach, hard. The six-shooter broke loose from Chum s desperate grip. But as it did, it fired.

Jim-Bob heard a man cry out. He looped a hard right fist to Chum's jaw and sent Chum spinning. Then he whirled around to see what had happened.

George Thorn sat on the ground, rocking back and forth in pain, gripping his leg. His teeth were gritted. With a sharp gasp, Sue-Ellen ran toward him. So did Jim-Bob.

Buster Fox got there first. Taking advantage of the confusion, he grabbed Sue-Ellen. He pulled her slim body up against him, his rough hands on her throat. "I got the girl, Jim-Bob. You can't shoot me without hittin' her. Now you throw me that gun of yours, or I'll go ahead and choke her."

It had all been too much for Jim-Bob. For a moment he stood there numb, wondering which way to jump.

Buster Fox didn't give him time to do much wondering. He tightened his grip on Sue-Ellen's throat. Jim-Bob could see her face coloring. "Throw me that gun now," Buster demanded again, "and stop foolin' around."

Jim-Bob's own .44 was still in its holster. He held Chum Lawton's six-shooter in his hand.

Sue-Ellen rasped, "Don't do it, Jim-Bob!" Buster's hands tightened, and she choked.

Jim-Bob couldn't take that. He said, "Here, Buster, take the gun," and he pitched it to the ground at Buster's feet.

Buster grinned malevolently. "Old Dencil needn't to've troubled himself. I took care of it myself."

Angrily Jim-Bob said, "Chokin' a girl half to death, you did. But you haven't got out of the country yet."

"You're not thinkin' you can stop me, are you, boy?"

Jim-Bob's heart sank at the thought of losing Buster Fox after all he had been through. "I'd almost rather have seen the lynch mob get you than see you go free."

"I told you all along you couldn't hold me, that it was just a matter of time."

"I wouldn't have lost you if it hadn't been for

that crazy Chum . . ."

He looked around for Chum and didn't see him. Chum had slipped away. "I'll come after you, Buster. I'll hunt you clear to Mexico if I have to."

"You come after me, boy, and they'll be measurin' you for a pine overcoat."

Buster was eyeing the gun Jim-Bob had pitched at his feet. He let go his hold on Sue-Ellen's neck and started to bend down, reaching for the gun with his manacled hands. Without turning, Sue-Ellen suddenly jabbed backward with her elbows. Buster clutched at his stomach, grunting in surprise. Sue-Ellen kicked the gun away from under foot, then jumped out of Buster's reach.

Jim-Bob had no time to think. Instinctively he leaped forward, drawing his gun as he moved. Buster dived at the one Sue-Ellen had kicked away. Jim-Bob swung the gunbarrel savagely. Buster's hat went rolling in the dust. Buster stiffened, but his fingers still groped for the weapon. His body awash with anger, Jim-Bob lashed out with the gunbarrel again. Buster groaned and sank to the ground on his belly. Holding the gun, Jim-Bob stood over him and gasped for breath. For a moment it was all he could do to keep from shooting Buster where he lay. But the wild tide of anger peaked, and he let the pistol go loose in his hand.

"You all right, Sue-Ellen?"

She had one hand on her throat, but she

nodded. "I'm sorry, Jim-Bob. I shouldn't have let him get so close."

"Not your fault. Your dad hit thataway, anybody would have done the same." Bitterly he remembered Tina Kendrick. "At least you fought him. You didn't just stand there and scream."

"Is that what Tina did?"

He nodded. "So far as I know, Buster never even touched her. She just stood there and screamed her head off."

Jim-Bob turned back to George Thorn, keeping an eye on the fallen outlaw. Buster didn't look as if he was going to get up for a while. "How hard are you hit, George?"

"I've had broncs do as bad, but I never did get to where I liked it." The bullet had torn through the high top of his right boot. Jim-Bob helped George to his feet. The old bronc stomper hopped to the edge of the porch with Jim-Bob propping him up. Jim-Bob caught hold of the boot and pulled it off. He found a small but steady flow of blood.

"Went through the flesh," George observed. His face was paling with growing shock. "Bet it'll be a good many days before I can ride a horse again. And it looks like I just lost a bronc rider." He motioned with his thumbless right hand. Jim-Bob heard a horse and glanced toward the corrals. Chum Lawton was just climbing up on the dun that had been saddled for Buster. Chum looked across at Jim-Bob, his face full of hatred.

The bronc made two or three crowhops, then stretched out down the south road in a lope.

Chum had left the gate wide open. Jim-Bob headed for the corral as hard as he could run. He got there just in time to throw up his hat and stop the other broncs from stampeding out into the open. Jim-Bob closed the gate. Sue-Ellen came up after him.

"Chum's gone after Tom Singleton," Jim-Bob guessed. "Bound and determined to earn him a little glory out of this someway. Looks like I better catch Buster another horse and vamoose *por allá*."

"Jim-Bob, you know there are three men up ahead somewhere, just waiting for you."

"And no tellin' how many of them behind, huntin' me."

"At least those behind aren't going to kill you."

"They're out to kill my prisoner. I don't intend to give them the chance."

"I can't talk you out of going on?"

He shook his head and roped out a black bronc.

Sue-Ellen clenched her hands, her mouth drawing thin. "Then promise me, Jim-Bob, that if those three men stop you, you won't do anything foolish. If they get you in a tight spot, let them have Buster Fox."

Jim-Bob threw a saddle on the bronc and carefully reached under for the girth, wary lest the black kick his head off. It was Chum's saddle, and Jim-Bob hoped it got torn up before the day was out. "They won't get him without a fight. If I let Buster Fox loose, I'm finished as a lawman. They'll run me out of town. I'll be lucky to get a job breakin' broncs."

"We'd rather have a live bronc rider than a dead deputy sheriff."

He finished drawing up the cinch and turned to face the girl. "Sue-Ellen, you've got no idea how long I dreamed and planned to get this badge. I don't aim to lose it. It means more to me than anything I've ever had."

"More even than life?"

He pondered a moment. "I don't know — maybe it does. I reckon I'll find out if it ever comes to where I've got to make a choice."

He saw tears squeeze into her eyes, and he caught her hand. Suddenly, somehow, he got some of the feeling he used to get when he was with Tina Kendrick, a funny tugging inside him.

"Look, Sue-Ellen, I'm not goin' to get myself killed. Fact of the matter, I expect I'll be back tonight, or maybe tomorrow, to see you. Why, I'll even take you to the next dance they throw at Sothern's, if it'll make you feel better about it."

She tried to smile. "Is that a promise, Jim-Bob?"

"It's a promise, and you can hold me to it."

There was something about her then, her pretty brown eyes, her open lips. On impulse he bent down and kissed her. He caught her by surprise, then her hands came up behind his arms and pressed tightly there while she warmly met his kiss. It was the first time Jim-Bob had ever seriously kissed a girl. All the blood seemed to rush to his head. He drew back, not understanding this sudden compelling urge that gripped him. His breath was short. His face was warm.

"I'll be back, Sue-Ellen."

He said nothing about it, but he knew George's wounded leg knocked out any chance that George or Sue-Ellen would try to tag along and help him. Badly as Jim-Bob wanted help, he was glad neither of them could go. He led the two horses back to the house. George still sat on the edge of the porch, gripping his leg. He had the bleeding stopped.

Jim-Bob asked, "George, you sure you'll make it all right?"

George nodded and dismissed him with a quick jerk of his head in the direction of Grafton. "You better get a move on."

Buster was sitting up, rubbing his head. Jim-Bob said harshly, "Get up from there, Buster. You don't know how close I came to killin' you."

Buster stared dumbly at his hand, streaked red from a gun gash on his head. His eyes were glassy at first. The haze slowly faded out of them. A searing anger took its place. "I swear, boy," he struggled for breath, "I'll kill you the first time I get the chance."

Jim-Bob's eyes narrowed. His voice was tight. "No, Buster, because the first time I think you're about to get the chance, I'll kill *you*."

He lifted Buster to his feet and led the black horse around. The horse had a little hump under the saddle, and that seemed to wake Buster up. A little shakily he gripped the reins up on the bronc's neck, getting a handful of mane with them. His right hand was on the horn. He swung up quickly, getting his right foot in the stirrup without losing any time about it. The pony goated a moment, then settled down.

Jim-Bob got on his sorrel. There was no sign of trouble. He looked down gratefully at George Thorn. "Thanks George, for everything."

Sue-Ellen was trying to fight down the tremor in her voice. "Remember your promise. I'll be lookin' forward to that dance."

Jim-Bob said, "I'll remember. We'll have us a time, you and me." Then he pitched the loop over the prisoner's head again. "All right, Buster. You lead."

It took a little while to get the kinks worked out of the two broncs. For a time it seemed that both of them were set with a hair trigger. They kept looking for the slightest excuse to break into pitching. Both Jim-Bob and Buster held the reins up tight. When either horse acted as if it was trying to get its head down to pitch, they firmly pulled it up again. The steady pace finally wore the foolishness out of the broncs.

All the way to the Thorn outfit, Jim-Bob had paused periodically to look and listen behind him. Now he was no longer so worried about his back trail as he was the one ahead of him. He pulled far away from the wagon road that led to Grafton. He preferred to strike out across country. He was careful not to top out over any rises that might outline them against the sky. He tried to keep to the lower ground, working in and out of the brush as much as he could.

"No use you tryin' all these shenanigans," Buster told him sullenly. "Old Dencil's goin' to find you anyway."

"Shut up, Buster." Jim-Bob's voice was sharp. Too sharp, for he knew he was letting Buster get under his skin too much. Now, for the first time since they had started from Swallowfork, Jim-Bob pulled out Mont's saddlegun and rode with it across his lap.

They rode two hours under the morning sun before they suddenly came upon a band of black-topped Merino sheep, grazing a green flat in the cool breeze. The sheep nearest them bolted back into the band. The excitement rushed through the entire bunch like the ripples on a disturbed hole of water.

"Let's back out a little and go around," Jim-Bob said. He could see the herder on the other side of the band, quickly sending his sheepdog out on the run to intercept those sheep which might flee from the flock on one side. Jim-Bob rode the other way to try to patch up that end. The sheep quieted, and Jim-Bob eased Buster toward the spot where the herder stood.

The sheep smell was strong around this grazing ground, yet it was not an unpleasant odor at all. Jim-Bob thought that if he lost Buster today, he might have to take up a job herding sheep. It might be all that was left open to him.

He recognized an old Mexican he had been seeing in this country occasionally for several years. *"Hola, amigo,"* he said. *"Como le va?"* He had picked up a little cow-camp Spanish in his time, as had most cowboys. It was enough to keep him from starving to death in Mexican country.

"Buenas dias," came the answer in the pleasant but formal manner which these people always showed to Angelos they didn't know well. The old *pastor* took in Jim-Bob's badge and his prisoner without any reaction showing on his gray-bearded face. *"Qué pasa,* sheriff?"

"I'm lookin' . . ." Jim-Bob started off, then remembered he wasn't talking Spanish. Some of these herders understood English, but they seldom admitted it. They often found ignorance, or the reputation therefor, to be their shield in event of trouble. *"Busco para tres hombres."* He knew he probably wasn't saying the words right, and he held up three fingers for the three men. He was reasonably sure the old Mexican wouldn't have seen the trio. He thought he probably had gotten far enough off the road to miss them.

But the herder smiled and told him yes, he had seen three men, and if Jim-Bob hurried, he probably could catch up with them. It had not been more than *una media hora,* half an hour, since they had passed this way. But before the young sheriff left, would he not care for some coffee? The three friends had paused with the herder. There was plenty, and surely the *patron* would bring more coffee before this was gone. Jim-Bob glanced at Buster Fox and saw triumph in Buster's gloating eyes.

Jim-Bob's stomach seemed to burn. Perhaps the coffee would help ease this sick feeling that welled up in him. *"Si, amigo,"* he spoke weakly. "I'll take some coffee."

The morning hours ground away. The summer heat grew, wrapping itself angrily around the two riders. The want of sleep was beginning to tell on Jim-Bob. He sweated, and his stomach was a boil from tension and sleeplessness. The steady riding, the constant watching, were relentlessly wearing him down. It came to him that he had been on the go since early yesterday morning.

Buster Fox was working on him, too. A mocking laughter was in his eyes. "What you lookin' so sharp yonderway for? You think Dencil's goin' to let you see him? He'll be up there someplace all right, only you'll never know till it's too late."

Edgily Jim-Bob said, "Why don't you quiet down?"

When Buster wasn't talking to him, roweling him with taunts, he was riding along humming tunelessly. That was just as bad.

Buster said, "Liable to come any time now, boy. See that clump of mesquite yonder? Dencil and old Hackberry and Pony might just be bellied down behind it, with their rifles trained on you this very minute. Or they might be waitin' just over that next hill. You don't know."

"I said shut up!"

"Tryin' to help you, boy, don't you know that? You ought to've realized by now that you ain't goin' to git me to Grafton. Why don't you just be sensible now and turn me loose? You can tell them Dencil took me. There won't nobody know the difference."

"*I'd* know, Buster." Jim-Bob's reddened eyes were constantly on the move, searching out every bush, every arroyo or cutbank.

"That girl back yonder," Buster said, "she's not a bad-lookin' one at that. Seemed to me like she thinks a right smart of you. You got her all wrapped up, I'd say. But what if somethin' happens to you boy? What's she goin' to do then? You want some other man to get her?"

Angrily Jim-Bob jerked on the rope. It went taut around Buster's belly, but Buster hauled up short. He didn't come out of the saddle this time. Face darkening, he gritted, "Go on then and be a fool. See what good glory does you when you're dead. It's goin' to pleasure me to get to pull the trigger on you."

Jim-Bob stopped often to lift his hat and wipe the sweat from his face, then to scan the country ahead of him. It seemed to him that he was sweating far more than Buster did. Always the shimmering heat waves put themselves in the way when he tried to get a good look. Occasionally he turned and glanced over his shoulder, wondering if Tom Singleton was closing the gap between them. All night he had dreaded the thought of Tom riding behind him, tall, gaunt, relentless as death. Somehow now he almost felt that he would welcome the sight of him.

But Jim-Bob saw nothing in either direction, nothing except the aimless scatter of brush. Cattle lay under many of the bushes, for at this time of year they usually grazed early, then shaded up from the heat of the sun. The cattle worried Jim-Bob. He had seen so many of them this morning that he was used to them. They moved, and he felt no alarm. But sooner or later there might be something under one of those bushes that wasn't cattle. It might be men. Would he glance over them and pass them by, or would he know the difference before it was too late?

Weakness grew, and his stomach was troubling him considerably. He took out the gold pocketwatch with John McClain's name engraved on the back. One o'clock now, past dinnertime. He felt that with a little something to eat he might do a bit better. He was glad now that George and Sue-Ellen had forced him to take time and have breakfast. Without that, he would be in real trouble by now.

They gradually moved closer to Grafton. Jim-Bob still hadn't seen anything. He began to feel a faint renewal of hope. There was a chance that they somehow had missed Dencil Fox. This was a big country. The outlaw couldn't watch it all. It was a slim chance, yet Jim-Bob clutched at it for support. Just ahead of them now ran a crooked creek. Beyond that, a couple of miles, lay Grafton.

"That creek sure does look good," Buster commenced. "I'm thirsty enough to spit dry dirt."

Jim-Bob moved slowly, his eyes cautiously working the fringe of green brush along the creekbank. He found himself also eager to reach the water, for he too was hot and thirsty, his clothes sweat-soaked. He knew the horses needed a drink. They hadn't had water since they had left the sheep camp. Jim-Bob gripped the rifle a little tighter as he watched the mesquite and catclaw. "Just go easy, Buster. Work down to the creek slow, and don't forget that rope or my rifle."

Something moved, far down the creek. Jim-Bob drew up abruptly, dropping low in the saddle and raising the rifle barrel, his heart tripping. His mouth went wide. He suddenly found himself gasping for breath. Then a calf moved out into the open. Jim-Bob lowered the rifle and straightened in the saddle. Relief washed through him, leaving him even weaker than he had been before. Buster chuckled, and Jim-Bob felt foolish. The two horses walked into the shallow water. Nowhere was the creek more than a couple of feet deep. Jim-Bob drew rein and looked around him. Seeing nothing amiss, he finally said, "We better let them drink." He slacked the reins. His horse dropped his head.

Then the quiet voice reached out to him from the brush. "Just take it easy, Jim-Bob!"

Chapter Eleven

Jim-Bob jerked erect in the saddle, hands desperately gripping the rifle. He saw Dencil Fox nonchalantly push his horse out of the mesquite on the far side of the creek and walk him up to the bank. Jim-Bob swung the rifle around to point at Dencil. Dencil had no gun in his hand, although there was one on his hip.

"You just as well put the gun down, Jim-Bob," Dencil said in a quiet, matter-of-fact way. "There's no use us havin' a fuss over this thing. You know you'd lose."

Jim-Bob found no voice for a reply. He heard Buster begin to laugh. The outlaw couldn't control himself. His laughter rose to a wild, high pitch. Only then did Jim-Bob realize how deeply worried Buster actually had been. The sudden wash of relief left Buster a-tremble.

Jim-Bob got settled enough to ask, "How did you find us?"

Dencil replied, "We been watchin' you more than an hour. We just kept edgin' along, out of your sight. We trotted ahead so we'd be here waitin' for you at the creek. This looked like the best place to do it. Now let Buster go, Jim-Bob, and we'll be on our way."

Still tight-gripping the rifle, Jim-Bob resolutely shook his head. He eased his horse up a little more, getting Buster between him and Dencil. "I've been through a lot since last night, Dencil, and come a long ways. I didn't do it just to turn Buster loose."

"You got no choice, Jim-Bob."

"I think I have. I've got a gun in my hand. You haven't. And I've still got hold of Buster."

Dencil smiled thinly. "I don't need a gun. I sort of came out to talk truce, you might say. Hackberry and Pony Sims are both in the brush, lookin' at you over the sights of their rifles. Now be sensible, button. Nobody wants to shoot you."

Furtively Jim-Bob looked around him. He saw nothing, but he knew Dencil was telling the truth. Pony and Hackberry were bound to be there somewhere. A tingle worked up and down his back. But he said stubbornly, "I'm comin' on, Dencil." He raised the muzzle of his rifle a fraction. "You better move aside."

Dencil shrugged regretfully. "I hate to have to play it this way, Jim-Bob. All right, Hackberry. Show him."

Jim-Bob saw the flash of the rifle at the instant a bullet smacked into the water right under his sorrel's nose. The bronc went straight up, then came down fighting. He pitched wildly, churning the water into an angry boil of mud. Jim-Bob's rifle went first, splashing and sinking out of sight. Jim-Bob made a vain effort to grab it and thereby lost his seat. He bounced once or twice behind the saddle. His right stirrup began to flop. Desperately reaching for any kind of hold, Jim-Bob accidentally raked a spur along the bronc's flank. The sorrel lunged harder, bawling as he jumped. This time Jim-Bob knew he was gone. He turned part way over in the air and came down on his back with a big splash.

Though he had lost the rifle, he hadn't lost his hold on the rope. At the sound of the shot, Buster Fox's horse also shied away. Seeing an opportunity for freedom, Buster put spurs to the black. But choking though he was in the muddy water, Jim-Bob saw the move coming. He got halfway to his feet and braced the rope across his hip.

The jolt knocked the feet out from under him, but Jim-Bob was up again almost instantly. Buster sailed out of the saddle. Crouching, Jim-Bob reached him in two long strides. He grabbed desperately at his holster and found to his vast relief that he had not lost the .44. He jerked Buster up against him and jabbed the six-shooter into Buster's ribs.

Buster was clawing at the rope. Jim-Bob caught hold of it and savagely jerked it taut again. "Back up with me, Buster," he breathed. "You're goin' to be my shield."

His eyes were afire from the water and mud. Wringing wet, his hat gone, his hair plastered down flat on his head, Jim-Bob began to drag

Buster back to the creekbank from which they had come.

Dencil Fox had pushed his horse out into the edge of the creek. Now he stopped again, staring in surprise at the suddenness with which Jim-Bob had recovered the advantage. "Don't shoot, Hackberry," he called to the man in the brush. Then, to Jim-Bob, "Use your head, boy. We got you dead to rights."

Jim-Bob glanced over his shoulder as he backed away, measuring the distance to the bank behind him. He kept moving, kept Buster up tight against him.

Buster rasped, "You're playin' the fool, boy. They'll kill you."

Jim-Bob clenched his teeth. "I swear, Buster, if they get me, I'll live long enough to blow your guts out!"

Buster yelled at the other men. "Get him clean and get him good, or he'll kill me!"

The three men held their fire. Dencil Fox had pulled back from the creekbank but still stood his horse there watching, perplexed. It was plain that he hadn't expected Jim-Bob to hold on like this.

Jim-Bob gritted, "All right now, let's run for it."

He and Buster broke into a trot, getting out of the water and moving up over the bank. At the last instant Jim-Bob gave Buster a hard shove that threw him off balance, temporardy helpless. Buster sprawled down the far side of the bank.

Jim-Bob came right behind him, keeping low, the gun in his hand. He caught Buster's shoulder and took a tight grip on it with one hand while he touched the muzzle of the gun to the man's head. "You just hold still, Buster. Act like you're dead, or I promise you *will* be!"

On his knees, Jim-Bob wiped a wet sleeve over his mud-streaked face. He wished for his hat. The sun in his unshaded eyes was forcing him to squint his eyes almost shut. He was not accustomed to being outdoors without a hat.

A growth of rank weeds at the top of the bank served as a screen so he could stick his head up far enough to see out. The broncs had settled down and stood across the creek. They had just as well be in New Mexico territory for what good they would be now, Jim-Bob thought.

Somberly he stared down at Buster. He still had his prisoner, but what was it worth to him now? He couldn't take him any place.

Dencil's voice came to him from across the creek. "It's just a matter of time. Don't make us have to come over and get you."

Jim-Bob's eyes still burned, but he had them blinked clear. He could see all right now. He wished for the rifle that had fallen in the creek. With that, he might be able to make a stand. But he still had his dad's old six-shooter. They might get him, but they'd know they'd been to a battle before they finished with it.

"Time's on my side, Dencil," Jim-Bob yelled. "Brother or no brother, you know Buster's earned everything that's comin' to him. If you rush me, he's liable to die too. And Tom Singleton's bunch is comin' up behind us, so you can't be rosin' any time. I've still got the upper hand. You better give Buster up and go yonderway before Tom gets here."

For a little while there was no answer, and Jim-Bob began to wonder if Dencil had slipped away, if he was up to something. But finally Dencil said loudly, "Did you ever have a brother, Jim-Bob?"

Jim-Bob replied, "No."

"Then you don't know how it is. We don't want to do it this way, Jim-Bob. But we've got to turn Buster loose."

Leaning against the cool, damp creekbank, Jim-Bob heard the horses. He stiffened, his heart missing a beat. He raised his head up. Two hundred yards up the creek, Pony Sims was splashing his horse over to Jim-Bob's side. Down the creek, Hackberry was doing likewise. Across, the two men turned at the same time. They bent low in their saddles and came spurring at Jim-Bob. A surge of panic, momentarily froze Jim-Bob. He wavered, knowing he couldn't stop both men. He might get one, but the other would surely ride him down. He remembered the promise he had made to Buster, that before he went down he would kill him. This was the time, he knew. But he couldn't do it.

He fired the six-shooter at Pony, knowing before he ever squeezed the trigger that he was going to miss. He raised up a little higher for a better shot. And that was his mistake. A white-hot streak of pain slashed through his right arm as the bullet caught him and spun him halfway around. The mesquites and the wet creekbank began to whirl about him. He made one feeble attempt to grip the gun that was slipping out of his fingers. It was no use. The gun fell. Jim-Bob stumbled and went down on his knees. He tried to grab the six-shooter again, but he could not make his fingers obey him. The life seemed to have gone out of them. He touched the gun but could not pick it up.

The riders were upon him then, Pony and Hackberry. They swung down from the saddles and brought their horses in close. One of them kicked the six-shooter out of the way. Jim-Bob heaved to his feet and lunged toward them, determined to fight. But the strength was not in him. A light-headedness seemed to take the legs out from under him, and he sank to the ground.

Gentle hands picked him up and set him on the edge of the creekbank. A grim-faced Dencil Fox laid down a smoking rifle and began tearing away Jim-Bob's bloody sleeve. "I hated to do it, Jim-Bob, I tell you I really did. I'd almost as soon have shot myself. Pony, run soak this handkerchief in the creek yonder, up there where the water's clean."

Dencil carefully went about washing the wounded arm. Slowly Jim-Bob felt some strength coming back to him. "Don't look like it chipped the bone any," Dencil said with evident relief. "It won't cripple you none, but it's apt to be awful sore for awhile."

Pony fished in Jim-Bob's pocket and got the key to the handcuffs.

Dencil said, "We'll take you and drop you off at the edge of Grafton, so somebody can get you to a doctor." He held the wet, cool cloth against the wound, trying to stanch the steady flow of blood. The wound was numb right now. Jim-Bob was aware only of a steady burning, and of the weakness that made his head so heavy.

Jim-Bob's voice was thin, but at least he found it. "I thought we'd shake you last night like we did the others. How did you know?"

"Just luck. We were waitin' out there in the dark like I told you we would. When we saw two men bust out the back door of the jail, we just naturally figured like everybody else that it was you and Buster. We went runnin' to help you. For just a second or two there, we got close enough that we could see those two men. Now, you might have fooled anybody else, but I knew my brother. I could tell at a glance that neither of them was him.

"So I asked myself a couple of questions, and the answers was easy. Those men were decoys. You and Buster was still in the jail. We worked up that way to get you as you came out, only you had already done it. The jail was empty.

"Your decoys rode south, takin' that mob with them. So I figured you'd probably head north with Buster. From there it was easy. Grafton was the logical place to go. We started out. We figured we were ahead of you all the way. We started scoutin' for you and finally spotted you an hour ago. We didn't think you'd put up the fight that you did."

Dencil smiled then, frank admiration in his bewhiskered face. I declare, Jim-Bob, you're the gamiest young rooster ever I seen. I hate to admit it, but you're goin' to make this country a real lawman. Tough, you losin' your first prisoner thisaway. But if folks haven't got sense enough to see what you're worth, I reckon it's their loss."

Soul-sick at the loss of Buster Fox, and physically sick from shock of the wound, Jim-Bob sat slackly, chin down. He had nothing to say. Dencil gently started to pull him to his feet. "Hackberry's bringin' the horses. Come on, we'll get you to town."

Buster Fox broke in roughly. "We ain't takin' him no-place, Dencil. I owe him aplenty, and I'm goin' to shoot him right where he is." He had picked up Jim-Bob's .44.

Dencil turned on him angrily. "Put that gun away, Buster. You've got no call to do this."

"No call?" Buster's voice lifted sharply. "You ought to see where he pistol-whipped me. You ought to see where he nearly choked me to death. You ought to hear the things he's said to me."

"Whatever he said, it couldn't have been any

worse than the truth. You likely had it all comin' to you, Buster."

"And he's fixin' to get what's comin' to *him*. Get out of the way, Dencil."

Jim-Bob stopped breathing. He sat helpless and watched the dark hatred boil up in Buster Fox's eyes. He looked into the muzzle of the beloved old gun his father had left him, he felt the cold hand of death grip his throat.

"No, Buster," Dencil shouted again and stepped protectively in front of Jim-Bob.

The gun roared. Dencil jerked and fell heavily against Jim-Bob. Jim-Bob tried to hold him, but he lacked the strength. Dencil folded and slipped out of his grasp.

Buster Fox stood with the smoking gun in his hand, staring stupidly down at his brother. "Dencil," he cried, "Dencil, what did you do?"

Jim-Bob knelt beside the fallen outlaw. Pony and Hackberry rushed to him. Gently they picked Dencil up and laid him down again, straightening his legs, smoothing the wet sand beneath him. Dencil's hand lay on his chest, where the lifeblood was slowly flowing out between his fingers.

Hackberry looked at the wound, then glanced up helplessly at Pony and Jim-Bob. His whiskered throat was suddenly active as he swallowed a couple of times. He slowly shook his head and dropped his chin.

Dencil's eyes were glazing, but he managed to find Buster. He looked up at his younger brother, his lips parting. Voice failed him at first. Then he whispered, "Buster, you just weren't worth it. Weren't worth it at-all . . ."

His head bobbed over.

Hackberry stood up and turned his back. Jim-Bob just stayed there on his knees, looking down at the bank robber who had died trying to save him. Relaxed as it was now, Dencil's face looked years younger. Strange how much he resembled Buster. A man who didn't know them well might easily make a mistake.

Jim-Bob lifted his gaze to Buster. He shouldn't have said anything, but anger moved him. "He may have looked like you, Buster, but that's the only way you were ever alike. He was worth a hundred of you."

Buster seemed to have been in a trance. Now Jim-Bob's voice tore him out of. "It was your fault!" he flared. "If it hadn't been for you . . ."

Buster remembered the gun in his hand, and once more he brought it up. Jim-Bob closed his eyes, knowing he was helpless against this. But he heard the metallic *clen-n-ch!* of a rifle lever and the hate-honed voice of Hackberry "Drop it, Buster, or I'll kill you!"

Buster whirled on Hackberry. "You double-crossin' . . ." Something in the man's eyes stopped him cold.

Hackberry said, "Just keep on talkin', Buster. I think I'd enjoy puttin' a bullet right through your thick skull."

Buster could not stand up to the icy stare. He

tried, but he began to tremble. He dropped the gun. Abruptly he turned on his heel and strode toward the black horse, which Hackberry had brought up just before the shooting. He stuck his foot into the stirrup and swung into the saddle. Urgently rowelling the animal the instant he had gained his seat, he broke into a lope.

Hackberry watched him a moment. Then he raised the rifle to his shoulder and squeezed the trigger. The black bronc jerked in mid-stride and dropped dead in its tracks. Jim-Bob expected to see Buster jump up and start to run. Then he realized, Buster was pinned helpless beneath the dead horse. Hackberry lowered the smoking rifle, his face twisted in satisfaction. "We tried to tell Dencil, but what can you say to a man about his own brother? He's all yours, Jim-Bob. See that he gets what he's got comin'."

Hackberry glanced at Pony Sims, then back at Jim-Bob. "All we ask of you is a good head start."

Jim-Bob nodded gratefully. "You'll have it."

The two men looked down at Dencil Fox. Hackberry sadly said, "I reckon we'll all wind up thisaway sooner or later. They always do, in our business. And it's all for nothin' — nothin' at-all. *Adiòs,* Jim-Bob."

"*Adiòs.*"

Jim-Bob stood and watched the two men ride away and disappear in the thick green brush. When they were gone, he leaned down and pulled Dencil's hat up over the still face. It was a painful effort for Jim-Bob to move around. Feeling was beginning to return to the wounded arm. He knew it wouldn't be long until he would be sick. He could hear Buster Fox groaning. He walked over and found the man lying helpless, one leg pinned under the black bronc's dead weight.

"Get me out of this, Jim-Bob," Buster pleaded. "It's heavy. It's killin' me, I tell you."

Jim-Bob watched him impassively. He made no move to help. "Maybe that'd be a good way for you to die."

Buster fought desperately, cursing as he did. But try though he might, he could not budge the leg. He struggled until his breath was gone and his face was almost purple Then he went stiff, listening. He looked up at Jim-Bob, a sudden fear crawling in his eyes. "You hear that, Jim-Bob? Horses. It's that lynch mob of yours, comin' to get me!"

"I don't hear anything." Jim-Bob really couldn't. There was a ringing in his ears.

"They're comin' though, I tell you, comin' to kill me! Jim-Bob, you got to get me out of here!"

Jim-Bob slowly shook his head. "I rode all night and half the day, tryin' to save you from that bunch. Now all of a sudden I'm sick to death of the whole thing. I don't care what happens to you."

Buster gasped. "You're a lawman. You got a responsibility."

Responsibility! What a word for Buster Fox to

use. Jim-Bob almost felt like spitting on him. "You've never known responsibility in your life. You've never felt obliged to anybody. Your own brother risked all he had to save you, and you killed him."

"I didn't mean to. But he's dead, and I'm alive. Jim-Bob, for God's sake, I want to *stay* alive. Get me out of here, please. I'll do anything, anything, I tell you!"

A thought came to Jim-Bob. "Even tell me where you hid the money you took out of the bank?"

"Sure. You get me out of here, and I'll tell you."

"You tell me first. Then maybe I'll get you out."

Buster was almost crying. His voice was breaking, and tears were beginning to course down his dusty cheeks. "Just before you-all caught up with me out there in that draw, I could tell it was all over. Remember that fence where I pulled the staples out of the posts and pushed the wire down so I could cross my horse over it?"

"I remember."

"There was a badger hole under one of them posts. I shoved the money into it and caved it in with my foot. I thought if I did get away, I could come back later and get it. And if I got caught, I might bargain my way clear with that money."

Jim-Bob said severely, "You'd better not be lyin' to me, Buster."

Buster cried, "I swear it's the truth, Jim-Bob.

You know where I crossed that fence. You can find the money easy. Now please, get me up from here. They're gettin' closer. I can hear them."

Jim-Bob picked up his handcuffs, his muddy .44 and the wet rope he had kept around Buster's waist. He caught his sorrel horse. He tried several times to get into the saddle, but he was too weak to make it. Giving that up, he led the horse over to Buster. He pitched the outlaw the loop end of the rope.

"Put that over your saddlehorn."

Buster did. Jim-Bob wrapped his end of the rope around his own saddlehorn and led his horse back. He tightened his cinch the best he could, then made his horse pull against the rope. It came taut once, then slipped back. Buster cried out at the weight falling on him again.

By now Jim-Bob could hear the horses coming, although he could not see them. He led the horse up again. This time he kept the animal pulling hard. He saw the dead bronc's body lift a little, then a bit more. He saw Buster strain. Suddenly then Buster was free and on his feet. He hobbled painfully, favoring the leg.

Holding his gun on Buster, Jim-Bob said, "We can't outrun them all the way into town anymore," he said. "I don't think I could even make the ride. But I got another idea. Let's get into that thick brush yonder."

Deep in the green mesquite, he found a tree

about the right size. "Flop down there on your belly."

Buster did. Jim-Bob made him stretch his hands out in front of him. He buckled one cuff around Buster's wrist, the other around the thick trunk of the tree. "You lay flat, and don't you even breathe," he warned Buster.

Jim-Bob led his horse back to the creekbank. He sat down exhausted beside Dencil Fox's body.

The riders broke out of the brush. Jim-Bob thought he counted ten men. Tom Singleton was in the lead. A lot fewer men than had started last night. Tom loped his horse up to Jim-Bob and stopped him. He quickly swung out of the saddle and dropped the reins, reaching Jim-Bob in three long strides. His stubbled face was tired, and trouble was in his dark eyes

"Jim-Bob, you all right?" He looked down at Jim-Bob's arm, and his mouth dropped open. The wound had begun to bleed again. Tom's voice was shaky. "We heard the shootin' from a long way off and came as fast as we could. How bad is it, boy?"

Jim-Bob's heart was beating rapidly. "I'll make out."

The other men swung down and gathered around. They, like Tom, were dusty and tired. Frowning, Tom examined the wound. "It's just a little way into Grafton. We'll take you to a doctor."

Thinking of Buster, Jim-Bob quickly said,

"No, Tom, I'll be all right. You-all can go on back. It's all over."

Tom knelt then and looked at the body. He lifted the hat, glanced briefly at the face, then covered it again. "Buster Fox?"

Jim-Bob only nodded. He didn't want to trust his voice in a lie.

"What happened?"

"Some friends of his tried to rescue him."

Tom looked away a moment. Jim-Bob gazed upon the men who had come with him. To his surprise, he saw relief come into their weary faces. It came to him that they were somehow glad the thing had been taken out of their hands.

Tom turned back, guilt in his face and in his voice. "Except for you gettin' hurt, Jim-Bob, I'm kind of glad it ended up this way. It's been a long night and a long day, and I've had plenty of time to think. A lot of the boys turned back. I found myself wishin' they all would, so I could too. Then we pulled up to the Thorn ranch this mornin', and that girl told us about those three men after you.

"She told us some things about ourselves, too. She told us if anything happened to you, it would be our fault. *My* fault. Funny, I always want to think of you and Dan as just kids. But you were one of the few real men in town last night, Jim-Bob. It was *me* that acted like a kid." Tom stared down at his feet and soberly rubbed the back of his neck. "You did real fine, Jim-Bob. Dan would've been proud of you. I don't expect he'd have found much to be proud of in me."

With his good hand Jim-Bob reached up and gripped Tom's arm. "He was always proud of you, Tom. I never blamed you, and Dan wouldn't have, either." Then he frowned. "Tom, do you mean you've gotten over the lynchin' fever? That if you'd caught up with us, you wouldn't have killed Buster Fox?"

Tom shrugged. "If we'd caught you early, we might have. But all mornin' I've just wanted to catch up with you and keep you from trouble with those men who were out to set Buster free."

Jim-Bob chewed his lip. He decided to take a chance. "If I told you this isn't really Buster, that I have Buster stashed away someplace, what would you do?"

Tom stared at him in puzzlement. "We'd help you take him wherever you wanted to go with him. He's your prisoner, and you've gone through a-plenty to prove it."

Jim-Bob studied Tom until he was sure Tom meant it. He could see remorse chewing away at the older man. He told Tom the truth about Buster. Tom grinned thinly at the end of the story and motioned for some of the men to fetch Buster in. Jim-Bob handed one of them the handcuff key.

Chum Lawton was with the men. He hadn't said anything. Now he stared incredulously at Tom. "You mean this is all you're goin' to do? You're just goin' to forgive him and go on? This is a chicken-hearted bunch if I ever saw one!"

Tom Singleton squared himself up to his full height. "Chum, I've listened to all I'm goin' to from you. If you want to fight with Jim-Bob, I'm sure he'll oblige you when he's able. If you want to fight with *me*, just keep on talkin'."

Chum swallowed and shut up. Nobody ever wanted to fight with Tom Singleton.

Jim-Bob said grimly, "Chum, the day this arm is well, I'm goin' to go lookin' for you."

Chum backed away, plainly wondering where he had gone wrong. The whole thing had blown up in his face, and he still wasn't sure how.

Buster Fox was crying like a child and pleading for mercy when they brought him back out of the brush. Jim-Bob looked away in disgust while Tom Singleton told the outlaw, "We're not goin' to hang you. We've decided to let the law handle that in its own due time."

Tom led Jim-Bob's horse up. "Come along, Jim-Bob. You need a doctor and a good long rest. You'll get them in Grafton."

Jim-Bob nodded. He was bone-tired, and the arm was beginning to throb. He wanted to throw himself across a bed and not get up for days.

"Tom," he said, "I know you're tired too and want to rest. But could you find somebody in Grafton that would ride back to Swallowfork and let Mont Naylor know everything turned out all right? And tell True Farrell I know where Buster hid the money. I'll dig it up as soon as I get back to Swallowfork."

"Sure, Jim-Bob."

Jim-Bob looked down. "One more thing, get him to go by way of the TX. Sue-Ellen will be sick to death with worry. I sure want her to know . . ."

Tom's hand was on the young deputy's shoulder, and his voice was warm. "A fresh horse will get a man there before dark. Anything particular you want him to say to her?"

Jim-Bob smiled weakly. "I don't reckon — yes, there is something. Just tell her a sore arm won't hurt my legs any. And she'd better not figure on dancin' with anybody but me!"